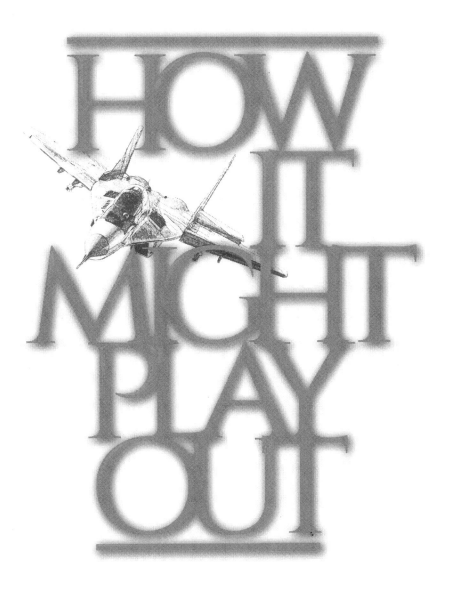

HOW IT MIGHT PLAY OUT

thirtysix.org

How It Might Play Out

How Current Events Could Lead to the Messianic Era

ISBN 9781796342987

Published by:
Thirtysix.org
22 Yitzchak Road
Telzstone, Kiryat Yearim
Israel   90838

אני מאמין **באמונה שלמה** בביאת המשיח, ואף על פי שיתמהמה עם כל זה אחכה לו בכל יום **שיבוא.**

י"ג עיקרי האמונה

I believe **with perfect faith** in the coming of Mashiach, and though he may tarry, nevertheless I will await him every day, **that he will come.**

13 Principles of Faith

Introduction

PART OF MY job, I feel, is to connect people to the concept of redemption. After all, one of the six questions the Talmud says people will be asked on their final day of judgment will be "Did you anticipate redemption?"[1] Sadly, many people will have to answer "no."

It's worse than that. NOT anticipating redemption slows it down, literally. Yes, the Final Redemption MUST come at a certain point, but it can also come earlier.[2] Although that may not sound like much of a reason to anticipate redemption from where we stand, because we AL-

---

[1] Shabbos 31a.
[2] Sanhedrin 98a.

READY have it so good, not anticipating redemption could become the very reason to make everything even worse.

Redemption is not only about being able to walk around freely and to safely live a Torah lifestyle. It's actually about much more than that, like returning the entire nation to its borders in all of Israel, everyone accepting Torah as from God, and perhaps most important of all, the return of the Temple with the Divine Presence in it. Until that time God "suffers," and for that reason WE should too.

The truth is that as good as we have it, we have NO idea what we are missing. It's a little like someone who thinks Saturday is the best day of the week until he discovers Shabbat. Then he wonders how he could ever have thought he was happy without it.

But try to tell that to someone who has never known Shabbat, the REAL Shabbat. More people become Torah observant because of Shabbat than for any other reason, but until they discover its great joy for themselves, it's hard for them to believe it. Until then, Shabbat just seems to restrict pleasure and fulfillment, not enhance them.

It also works like that with respect to redemption. When things are going well for the

Jews, they think they're already living it. They don't believe that life can get any better, and they're not convinced just by someone saying that it will, at least not enough to motivate them to anticipate and expedite it.

That's one of the main reasons we've never really been ready for the end of an exile. It usually catches most Jews off guard, even the ones who pray for redemption three times a day. They just don't see it coming because they didn't see how current events could and would evolve into end-of-exile events—until they actually did. And they STILL can't see it today.

To try to do something about that, I started a weekly essay called "Connecting the Dots." The goal was to paint current events in messianic terms, in order to get people thinking that way. More than likely it only worked for the people who already thought that way, or at least wanted to, and not for those who didn't.

For a few months in 2015 I went from the essay format to a novel format. I decided to portray the End-of-Days once again. I had already written two novels about this, called "Not Just Another Scenario, 1 and 2. I called the new novel "How It Might Play Out," showing how the events of that time could lead to an End-of-Days' scenario to stimulate the imagination of my readers.

I have no idea how many people read it or liked it. I do know that my mailing list increased more during those months than at other times. People love a good story, and some people like a messianic story even more.

A short while later I finished the novel. I felt the story had ended, and that it was time to go back to the essay format, which I did. "How It Might Play Out" was archived, and I forgot about it.

Several years later it occurred to me to give the material a second look. Perhaps it was still relevant. Maybe it was even publishable. I decided that it was, and here it is, published. At the very least, it may help those willing to think about Mashiach to do so, and thus be able to answer on their day of judgment, "Yes, I DID anticipate redemption."

After all, we're certainly living in the Messianic Era, probably towards the end of it. SURPRISE![3] So we might as well get with the program before the program moves along without us. That's never worked well for us in the past.

---

[3] See my books "Talking About the End-of-Days" and "Need to Know" for substantial proof of that.

TO THE OUTSIDE world the cloud surrounding the mountain was something to watch in wonder and to photograph. It was but a single cloud, encompassing a single mountain, but the lightning and thunder coming out of it made it seem so unusual, so...biblical. It was as if the mountain had its own weather system. In moments, the shot was on its way around the world via social media.

The Egyptian soldiers also noticed the strange phenomenon. Some took it as a sign that Allah was blessing their attack. A few others weren't so sure, especially the ones who recalled that, according to Jewish tradition, the Jewish people had received their Torah from the top of some unknown mountain in that area. It made them feel eerie, very eerie, especially as they moved their divisions into position along the Israeli border.

Had they seen the person climbing the mountain earlier that day, they might have really wondered what was happening on top of the mountain. They certainly would have wondered how anyone could possibly survive such a fierce localized storm, not knowing that all was calm in the eye of the "hurricane."

* * *

As he stood there on top of the mountain, he was completely oblivious of the world outside the cloud. Feeling supported without any form of support, it was if he were lying down while standing up. Every part of him seemed given over to the control of another, or rather to Another.

Images flashed through his mind. His eyes were closed but he saw perfectly. It was as if a movie were playing in his mind's eye: the history of Jewish suffering and exile from the beginning until the present. It was a crash course in Jewish history, the painful side of Jewish history. It was overwhelming.

There was a voice, although his ears heard

nothing. The voice spoke to him and it reassured him. Although he felt despair, it comforted him. He was witnessing more hardship than any one person had ever seen, but the voice told him that all would be rectified. It told him that it was all part of his developmental process, and that it would empower him to save his nation in ways that it had never before been saved. He felt the ongoing change, a remarkable transformation.

Miles away the situation was totally different. A major storm was developing there, but of a very different nature.

* * *

Standing on top of his Mark IV Merkavah tank, the young Israeli officer scanned the scene in the distance with his binoculars and confirmed the worst. The enemy had already amassed troops and state-of-the art artillery north and south along the Israeli border, as far as he could see with his binoculars.

The math was simple.

The Israeli army was horrifyingly outnumbered and terrifyingly outgunned.

Again.

There was a difference this time, though. A big difference. In the past it was 10 or more Arabs to every Jewish soldier. There may have been Russian advisors working behind the scenes, but it was Arab soldiers they confronted. There may have been Russian MiGs flying, but it was Arabs who piloted them. That had been an advantage.

Not this time though. This time there was an international force facing them. In this war they were about to fight against the best of the best. The international army was massive, extremely well-equipped, and very well-advised. The situation was impossible for the Jewish army, logically speaking.

After the UN vote in 1948 to allow Israel to join the "family of nations," the Brisker Rav was quoted as saying that the United Nations had come into existence just for this purpose. Ironically, it was the UN that now threatened the very existence of the Jewish state.

It was obvious to everyone that there was no way to beat the enemy through conventional means. For the Israelis it was a case of holding out as long as possible, while hoping for a miracle that would allow them to survive without having to use their nuclear arsenal. While such a counterattack might obliterate the enemy, the Jewish state would not fare much better.

For the UN army it was a question of ending the war quickly. The plan was to disarm the Israeli army before a nuclear strike was even possible. They knew where the bombs were and how they would be delivered. Their technology enabled them to pin down the IAF and deny it any opportunity to use its lethal load. Quite frankly the top brass wondered why the Israelis didn't just call it quits before anything even started.

"Jewish chutzpah knows no bounds!" one UN general said to another.

* * *

From his foxhole Sergeant Yoav Baruch had a front row seat at the End-of-Days. He was an observant Jew and believed in such things as the "War of Gog and Magog." Scanning the enemy in front of him with binoculars, he had never felt so hopeless. He lowered his "glasses" and, taking a few deep breaths, told himself, "It's in times like these that we get to prove our trust in our Creator."

Although his fellow soldiers shared his sense of despair, not all of them shared his religious outlook. Their thoughts were more about how their dreams of completing university degrees or starting up businesses to quickly make millions of dollars were about to go poof. Instead of their dreams, their worse nightmares were about to unfold, and with them the end to their very short lives.

* * *

"There are entire battalions to the north, south, east, and even to the west," the general told the Israeli Prime Minister. "They have all sides covered, including the sea."

The PM said nothing. He sat there with folded hands holding up his head and covering the lower part of his face. He digested the intel and it made him nauseous. He was with his best military advisors and most talented strategists, but they were surrounded by a massive and formidable enemy army, ready to attack at a moment's notice. As much as they had anticipated this moment, they were still unprepared for it.

"God help us," was all the PM could say. "God help us all."

It was not what the generals had wanted to hear, but they wondered if it had become the only real answer to the problem. "No atheists in a foxhole," one sardonically thought to himself.

* * *

Many Western leaders felt that the Israelis had had this coming to them for a long time. "Is it really that difficult for them to grant the Palestinians statehood?" they asked themselves. "Are they so paranoid about their security that they are prepared to risk everything just to prevent a Palestinian state?" they wondered. "This war will teach them a lesson," they claimed. "It will give the Palestinians what is rightfully theirs and put the Israelis, whatever remains of them, on the receiving end."

Not every leader was this blind or biased. Some knew in their heart of hearts that the Israelis had a point. They found themselves sympathizing with the Israeli people, but not enough to stand up to the rest of the Western world. They had their own countries and political careers to worry about. Without question the Arabs were a problem, but not theirs. Not yet, at least.

The American President was not one of the Israeli sympathizers. As he stared out the window of the Oval Office, his back to his staff as they discussed strategy, he admired the perfectly manicured White House lawn. He also imagined giving a speech there in the very near future about the new world he helped to create. He would mourn the loss of the Jewish state, a least to those listening, and assure everyone that the "new world order" would advance the cause of civilization as never before.

He told himself that just as the lawn before

him lacked any weeds whatsoever, it was time that the world did as well.

In his final months in office he had worked hard to convince his fellow Americans, especially the Jewish ones, that he had done everything in his power to make peace in the Middle East. He went out of his way to make it look as if he really wanted the Jewish state to continue, and as if it were the Israeli leadership that had forced his hand. There would definitely be some fall-out, but the American Jewish population made up only two percent of the total population, if that. The situation would be manageable.

The president also knew this because some local Jewish leaders, who shared his vision of the future world, told him that most American Jews no longer sided with the Jewish state. If it weren't prepared to exist the way they wanted it to exist and needed it to exist, then it need not exist at all, they argued. They quietly backed the president, and promised to help with damage control after the inevitable result.

They even anticipated the shift of Jewish leadership from Jerusalem to Washington once the Jewish dust settled. If they believed in the concept of a Final Redemption, it was in the Diaspora, to which they had become so accustomed. "It had served them well until this point," they mused among themselves, "and it would serve them even better after the fall of the Jewish state," they confidently concluded.

* * *

The history lesson was coming to a close. He knew for sure because the images were becoming increasingly current. He had always felt a great love for God and His people, but now it was even more intense. It was as if he could feel the collective pain of hundreds of generations of suffering Jews. In the past so much negative emotion would have overwhelmed him. Now it only seemed to strengthen him.

Something told him to open his eyes. He had forgotten that they were closed because he was able to see so much with his mind's eye. He had not even been aware of the cloud swirling around him on the mountain. And although it may have appeared dark like a storm cloud on the outside, it was perfectly white and heavenly on the inside.

Suddenly the cloud began to open up before him! He was able to see with his eyes but much farther than ever before. He could see the current situation all along the borders of Israel. Not only was he able to see the battle unfolding, he could also sense what each side was feeling.

Fear, doubt, arrogance, confusion...there were so many different emotions being felt by many different people all at the same time. But he also could sense some serenity...some belief...some trust. Apparently there were people out there who were relieved by the current direction of events, believing that the final act of an evil-filled history was at last coming to an end.

It truly was.

IT WAS TWO days before Shavuot, the holiday that recalls and celebrates God's giving His Torah to the Jewish people. To mark the occasion some eat dairy, often cheesecake, prior to the main holiday meat meal. Others have a completely dairy meal although they usually eat meat on holidays. Both traditions recall that Shavuot was the time in history when the Jewish people received and accepted the 613 mitzvot, one of which is to not eat milk and meat together.

Another Shavuot tradition is to remain awake all night learning Torah. Tradition teaches that the Jewish people overslept when the Torah was given at Mt. Sinai. To avoid the same error, we try to stay awake the entire night and learn Torah.

There is even a special "tikun" that was compiled specifically for the night of Shavuot.

Yoav could still taste his mother's cheese-cake, or so he thought. It was almost a year later now and he was in a six-foot-deep hole. He wasn't dead, but rather armed and ready for the worst. He tried to shake off the memory because it wasn't a moment for daydreaming and reminiscing. It might be the last day of his life, and surely would be if he failed to remain focused on the mission at hand.

As he tried to bring himself back to the present, a present that he would much prefer to avoid, he recalled that King David, the ancestor of Mashiach, had died on Shavuot day. "Wouldn't it be ironic," he thought to himself, "if I died on the same day?" Then snapping out of his reverie, he berated himself, "No, it wouldn't! It would be more ironic if I survived on the same day!"

"Talking to yourself again?" his friend teased while watching the enemy in the distance through his gun scope.

"No one else to talk to," Yoav teased back.

His friend smiled to himself.

There was a moment of silence as each soldier tended to his own business.

As Yoav checked his weapon, he said, "You know, they say that the Final Redemption will begin on Pesach and end on Shavuot."

Still squinting through the scope, the other answered, "They who?"

He locked and loaded. "They...you know...the rabbis," he said matter-of-factly, knowing that his words would get his friend's goat.

The second soldier shifted his eyes from the scope and looked at his friend. "The only thing that may end now is our life," he said. Then he added, as if to strip Yoav of all hope, "Look out there! Does THAT look like redemption to you?"

No answer.

"Maybe it is for them," he finished, "but certainly not for us."

Silence.

"I just hope that it will be quick and painless when it happens."

"Yeah, well I believe in miracles," Yoav shot back. "The redemption can come in the blink of an eye. Why, just last week..."

"Please don't," his friend pleaded, cutting him off mid-sentence. "I really hate delusional thinking. It makes me delusional too. If you want to believe in fairy tales, that's your business. It's not my business."

"Fairy tales!" Yoav mockingly said. "Well, I'm just letting you know now that I reserve the right to say 'I told you so' after the impossible happens."

"IF it happens…" his agnostic friend said.

"They say that there are no atheists in a foxhole," he quipped, "but last time I checked, we're up to our eyeballs in one."

"There are no atheists in a foxhole," his friend defended himself, "because they all get picked off by snipers while having useless conversations like this one!"

With that he went back to scanning the enemy lines through his gun scope. Yoav had the last word though, saying, "That was BECAUSE they were atheists."

* * *

To be on top of Mt. Sinai more than 3300 years after the Torah was given was overwhelming, and that was an understatement. The mountain had been asleep for the entire time. Now it was awake again, as if it had a life of its own. It was hard for him to leave it.

It was also hard to believe. Last year at this time he was sitting in a Beit Midrash, giving a shiur. On Shavuot night that year he was awake the whole night, saying the tikun and inspiring the boys of his yeshivah to stay up and learn as well. He would never have believed that one year later he'd be at the place the Torah was actually given.

He would never have believed that one year later the Messianic Era would actually begin, and that he would be instrumental in bringing it about.

Then again, he was not the same person he had been a year ago. Well, perhaps he was the same person, but on a much higher level, and not just physically. He had worked hard on himself the past year, committing to new levels of self-sacrifice for his Creator and His Torah. Apparently it had a greater impact on his life than he had imagined.

He just knew things. It wasn't as if he were talking to God or even hearing His voice in his head. Yet he seemed to know exactly what God was thinking and what he himself needed to do next. For example, he knew that it was time to descend the mountain. He knew that his mission had already begun. He could feel the tension miles away, but he still didn't know how he was meant to resolve it. He also knew that he had to wait to find out. When the time came, something seemed to tell him, he would know what to do.

His questions seemed to get answered almost as fast as he thought of them.

* * *

It was the toughest moral decision of his entire life, not just his political career. People had always said that if Israel were going to go down, it would take the world with it, or at least as much of it as possible. It was no secret, although it was treated like one, that the Israelis had hundreds of nuclear bombs ready to go. The only question was whether or not they would use them. Would they really use them?

After all, it wasn't only a question of launching them. Satellite reconnaissance knew every Israeli military move in real time, even underground. Enemy missiles were aimed and ready to strike within seconds. Planes were ready to shoot down anything remotely Jewish. The Israelis had the goods, many thought, but no viable way to use them.

However, if ever necessity were the mother of invention and innovation, it was in Israel. The need to survive against tremendous odds and countless enemies made incredible demands upon Jewish leaders to anticipate difficult situations well in advance so that solutions would already be in place by the time they were needed. Continued existence depended upon it.

It took a lot of time, more than 10 years, but patience and perseverance paid off. Israeli intelligence took advantage of friendly governments to prepare for the time when less friendly leaders might take office. Operation "Sitting Duck" had been completed over a decade ago; supposedly "undeliverable" nukes were already assembled and in position in key cities around the world.

There had been one major scare though. Investigative journalists sometimes really get in the way. Ever since Watergate many tried to break the big story, and maybe even pick up a Pulitzer Prize along the way. It cost some their life instead.

It just goes to show that if you poke around long enough, clues about any secret are bound to surface. Well, one journalist poked into a rumored Israeli program that placed secret nuclear devices in major cities around the world. "Loose lips sink ships," and some Israeli loose lips almost sunk Sitting Duck. It took some serious espionage and expensive false leads to shake the guy off the track and make him lose the scent. Had he not given up, that may not have been the only thing he would have lost.

* * *

"I know there is a protocol that pinpoints when it becomes time to use them," the Israeli Prime Minister addressed the top Israeli brass, "but is it still relevant? The world has changed a lot since it was written."

"Up to date," was all the general said.

The prime minister paused and contemplated his next question. He already knew the answer he had just received. Asking for it was simply a stall tactic. He drew a deep and contemplative breath.

"Do we do something like this?" he asked.

There was a palpable silence in the room as they considered the words. It was unprecedented that with eight high-ranking officials in the room, all that could be heard was breathing. Then finally a response.

"It's a defensive measure," another general said. "I don't see what option we have."

"I mean…" the prime minister continued with caution. Just asking the question could have major military repercussions, and therefore major political repercussions. The last thing the country needed at such a critical moment was a change of leadership. "I mean, is this something we—the Jewish people—do? Do we wipe out millions of innocent people just because millions of our innocent people are being wiped out?"

The PM scanned the faces of those around him. Even poker faces reveal something about the insides of people, especially when they're caught off-guard. The eyes betray their innermost sentiments without them even being aware of it. Judging from the eyes and the faces of those looking at him, the PM sensed their own doubt, and their resentment for his having brought it so close to the surface. Military personnel can afford no cracks.

"Well, hopefully," a voice emerged from the back of the room, "we won't need to answer that question."

No one turned around to see the source of the voice because it was easily recognizable. "If I'm not mistaken," the elder statesman continued, "Operation Sitting Duck from the beginning was meant only as a bluff, a way to intimidate the would-be powers at the time to save Israel from extinction. I don't think the people who set it up ever intended that we would actually go ahead and use it."

"So you would rather let our last line of defense remain unused as all of us bite the proverbial bullet?" the PM's right-hand man asked sarcastically. Although he was half his age, he had twice the chutzpah.

The statesman smiled. "Do you know the story of Samson?" he asked the dissenter.

"What, the one from the Bible? Of course I do!" he answered impatiently, as if they had time for such nonsense.

"And do you know the difference between what Samson did when he killed all the bad guys around him, and what you plan to do?" he continued.

He did not know which answer his antagonist was looking for. He had played mental chess with him before and lost just about every time. His silence, however, made him even more vulnerable, and he felt it.

The statesman continued. "Samson asked for and received God's permission to kill the Philistines, who were comparable to the Palestinians of our time. Unless you know something I don't..." He paused for a moment. He wanted to add the words, "which is highly doubtful." However, it wasn't the right moment to be childish, so he ended by saying, "We have yet to receive God's permission to commit mass murder, and on a global scale yet."

Another pause.

"If and when we do," he ended, "then we can stop having this discussion and just go ahead with Sitting Duck."

"God?" a new and frustrated voice said, entering the fray. "You bring God into this discussion when He, if He even exists or cares, has allowed us to reach this point?"

Incredible as it was, a philosophical debate began that would last a full five minutes. The prime minister, however, didn't get involved because he was absorbed in a message he had just received. No name was attached to it, and it wasn't traceable. No one, except the prime minister himself and the head of the Mossad, knew whom it was from. If word ever got out who actually sent it, the political fallout itself would be nuclear.

The message was short and clear:

Full attack 0-600 hours.

It was already 0-700 hours, which meant that the attack was going to begin the next morning, Erev Shavuot. It was one week earlier than anticipated, and this time it was the PM's face that was guilty of betrayal. Out of the complete silence came only one word: "When?"

As if to answer the question, phones frantically started ringing all over the room.

* * *

He had no idea of the power he could or would access. In the meantime, he just continued down the mountain. For all intents and purposes he felt every bit as human as he had felt the previous week. Although he had experienced the supernatural, he had yet to use it on command.

Something inside him wanted to test the water, but at the same time something else told him, "Not yet."

All he knew at that point was that the world, after thousands of years of waiting, was about to cross the threshold into an entirely new and different period of time. Theory was fast becoming fact and even he had difficulty adjusting to that. However, he noticed that he was strangely calm about the entire matter. He assumed that was a good thing.

3
B'emunah

JEWS AND POVERTY often go together. Jews and the poverty of other people do not. In fact, one of the warning signs that it is dangerous for Jews to live somewhere in the Diaspora is its level of poverty. Countless times throughout history poverty has brought out the worst in people, sometimes compelling them to vote for extremist leaders, sometimes making antisemitism more likely and the mistreatment of Jews more acceptable. Poverty makes people angry and angry people need scapegoats.

One reason the signs of change were blurry this time was because they were hidden behind subterfuge. In the 1930s it was impossible to hide the economic depression because people were no longer able to buy on credit and soup kitchens were out in the open. When the Great Depression of the 1930s came, everyone knew about it, and it killed consumer confidence.

Since then no phrase has probably resulted in as much falsehood and fudging as "consumer confidence." Healthy economies need healthy consumer spending, which requires at least the appearance of a healthy economy. This in turn requires consumer confidence, something that, once lost, is not easy to restore. It can take years of prosperity before people feel comfortable enough to let go of their hard-earned cash.

This has taught governments to do whatever they can to project the impression that the economy is doing well, even when it isn't. This way the average guy in the street doesn't get cold financial feet and hoard his money, which would really sink the economy. The unspoken motto has become "consumer confidence at all cost."

It creates what might be called a "smoke-and-mirrors" economy. Money is tight? Print more of it. Unemployment is high? Change the standard of measurement so that actual double-digit unemployment can be made to look like single-digit unemployment. This enables people to go to bed at night, wake up the next morning, go to work, and spend the money they make.

However, as with most things in life, you can run away but you can't hide, at least not forever. Truth inevitably has a way of catching up with us. Besides, in a country with hundreds of millions of people, it is hard to keep a secret forever. Someone is bound to notice the truth about the economy and someone else is going to be willing, even encouraged, to report the truth to the rest of the world.

How much more so will this be the case when financial growth occurs only for the wealthy ten percent of the population. You can't expect the other 90 percent to financially stagnate and not rebel. Poverty breeds anger, and anger breeds revolt.

It already has.

The flash points may have been race-related, but the anger that was ignited had been building from years of financial frustration. Usually where there is smoke, there is fire. In this case it means that where there is poverty and frustration, someone will have to play the role of the scapegoat, because angry and frustrated people need to vent. They need to express their frustration. They feel cheated and they need to take revenge against those who cheated them, or at least against those they want to believe cheated them.

The wealthy for their part thought they could

buy all the security they needed to protect themselves against angry mobs. They also assumed that since the government was so technologically advanced, it could keep the crowds at bay. Incredibly rich and very well-connected, they figured they could weather the storm that everyone around them was suffering from.

The smarter ones got out while it was safe to do so. They went to secure places where they could not be found or targeted by the people from whom they made their money. They made sure that when the banks collapsed, as most of them did, they were set for life in the "safe house" they had set up long before.

But God runs the world, not the wealthy. Some get confused about that, which is why God makes a point of straightening them out.

When history still had time left before ending, it was possible to escape divine judgment, at least for a while. Many of the rich escaped World War II, at least financially. Many even became richer because of it, and went on to expand their empires during more peaceful times.

Now, however, history had run out. The next period was going to be completely different, messianic. Entrance was by divine invitation only. There was no sneaking in, no paying off the "doorman." Many would survive the transition but many would not. This time it didn't matter how much money a person earned, but rather how much merit he had accumulated, not in his bank account, but in the eyes of God.

If Jews had just taken the time to learn their history, they would have been able to read the writing on the wall. It was in block letters that screamed out, "LEAVE! NOW!" They even had a homeland to go to this time, and yet so many waited until it was too late to get out. Once again they missed the opportunity to do what they could and should have done earlier.

What is it about the Jewish people that makes us throw caution to the wind? Why do we always believe that the current generation of anti-semites is more civilized than previous genera-tions of Jew haters? Why do so many of us bank on the possibility that, as bad as things get, they will still be endurable? Is it just hope? Over-in-vestment in foreign lands? A fear of change? Or just plain ignorance and short-sightedness?

Many Diaspora Jews have probably asked themselves the same questions over the ages when, like so many before them, they woke up too late and realized that they had bet on the wrong outcome. Risk looks entirely different when you're looking down the barrel of a gun from the wrong end.

Part of the problem is that psychology plays such a big part in our life and our decisions, often putting us at great risk. A man gets elected to public office and does something wrong, but the public refuses to see his sin for what it is because they don't see him as a sinner. Maybe he made a mistake, or got careless, or acted a little selfishly. But that doesn't make him a danger to the Jewish people, does it?

It becomes even more complicated when such a person projects a good persona. If he creates a positive image, or at least one that people are comfortable with or attracted to, they'll go with the image rather than the reality of the record. Supporters will rationalize the evils of those they promote until the situation becomes so incredibly wrong that even they can't deny their error.

The American Jewish population should have started murmuring the moment the new president reached out to the Arab world and apologized for America's role in peacekeeping around the world. They should have realized that, as much as the American leader kept telling Jews that he was committed to the survival of Israel, he may not have envisioned Israeli survival quite the same way that Jews do.

And when he spurned the Israeli prime minister, who only wanted to secure his country and the world against evil nuclear powers, Jewish communities around the country and the world should have raised their voices. They should not have sat back and waited to see how things would play out, because by the time they realized they should cry, "Foul!" it would be too late both for Israel and for them.

Furthermore, when the American leader, against the wisdom of those who knew better, bent over backwards to appease Iran, abandoning the Arab ally Saudi Arabia along the way, Jews should have started making escape plans. They should not have merely pondered whether or not Europe of the 1940s could become America of the 2000s. They should have taken past precedent seriously and simply assumed that "better safe than sorry" is the best motto.

However, people who grow up with a particular psychological outlook often have a tough time switching to another one later on in life. Cognitive dissonance is a much easier alternative in the short run, although it too often leads to deadly ends. When all is said and done, it is painfully difficult to change the way people look at reality, especially if they are used to enjoying their own reality.

* * *

"I never imagined this would happen, not today, not in America."

Arthur Daniels was a businessman, a very successful businessman. He was 69 years old and had been head of a Fortune 500 company. He built it up from scratch the honest way. Although he started with nothing, coming from a poor Jewish family that arrived from Europe after the war, he was a hard worker with a fair bit of intelligence. With some luck, he managed to start his own business by the age of 27.

One thing led to another, opportunities led to other opportunities, and Arthur took advantage of them all. But he prided himself on always doing things legally and with integrity. On several occasions it was almost at the cost of his success, but he stuck with it and in the end it worked in his favor.

He had never been one to parade his wealth. He didn't deny himself what he could afford but he tried to keep it on an even keel. Nevertheless, he was certainly accustomed to much better accommodations than the ones he was presently sharing with others, also Jewish but of different economic classes. He wasn't religious by any stretch of the imagination, and was offended by the way he was being treated. He repeated his words to himself, "I never imagined this would happen, not today, not in America."

He didn't realize that he had vocalized his thoughts but he had, and he was overheard. Although not a business success of the caliber of Mr. Daniels, Harry Moskowitz was one in his own right.

"Which one of us did?" he asked Daniels.

"Pardon me?" he replied, not realizing that someone was responding to his comment.

"Which one us did?" Moskowitz repeated, assuming he just hadn't been heard.

"Which one of us did what?" Daniels continued, not sure what his "roommate" was referring to.

It finally occurred to Moskowitz that Daniels didn't know that he had been overheard.

"Like what you said," he replied matter-of-factly. "Which one of us ever thought that we'd be shipped off to 'camps' in the good old US of A?

Daniels allowed a smile to escape, his first in days, at hearing the term "US of A." He hadn't heard that expression in a long time. He knew what Moskowitz meant about the camps. What Jew wouldn't? But he refused to accept the comparison and said, also matter-of-factly, as if by appearing calm things would calm down, "We were hardly 'shipped off to camps.' We came by Amtrak and government transport, not stuffed into cattle cars. They even had," he said with obvious disgust, "kosher food...for those who still believe in that kind of stuff. We sat on comfortable chairs, and," he said, looking around the large room and motioning with his hand, "this is not a 'camp,'" pausing for a moment as he considered just how bad the situation was, and then qualifying, "at least not like the one my parents were sent to back in the 1940s."

"Humph!" was all Moskowitz said. It was all he had to say because it said everything, given the situation facing the Jews in hundreds of internment camps throughout the United States of America. On one hand their conditions were much better than those of the Jews of the Holocaust or of the Japanese after the attack on Pearl Harbor. On the other hand...

Some things were quite clear to just about everyone. They may have been "detained" for their own protection against the angry mobs, but they were not free to come and go as they pleased. They were not exactly prisoners, yet they were in secured areas surrounded by armed guards. The US government was "taking care" of them but it was unclear for what end. They were totally cut off from the outside world, hidden away in secret locations around the country. If they were to go missing, Daniels thought to himself, who would know? It sent a chill down his spine.

It seems that Daniels and Moskowitz had the same thought because simultaneously they began to scan the cavernous room, starting from opposite directions. Slowly they turned their heads towards each other and eventually found themselves looking into each other's eyes. How uncomfortable it felt! It was if their souls were bared before each other.

They immediately looked away, but each knew what the other was thinking, and that it was the truth: They were never going home again. What they had accomplished during their lifetime would be wiped away, and now there was even a good chance that they too would disappear from history without a trace. The money they saved and all the hours they spent working were for nothing. Now they, like so many others around them, couldn't even buy a can of soda had they wanted to, let alone escape to freedom.

They hadn't the slightest clue about the idea of a savior, of Mashiach, or that in the near future there might be an even more dramatic change. As they despaired, they had no inkling that within a single moment everything could—and would— change in ways they believed could happen only in the movies.

JERUSALEM. THE ETERNAL capital of the Jewish people. Well, at least it is to the Jewish people. Apparently others begged to differ, and they were willing to go to war about it—which they did.

There had been murmurings for decades, but people balked. Christians claimed parts of the Old City for themselves, but only behind the scenes. The Arabs did it out in the open and were largely ignored. It wasn't until the US Supreme Court decided in favor of the president, who once again catered to the "other side" by pushing for the internationalization of the holy Jewish capital, that the reality of the situation began to settle in.

It was also major chutzpah. How does one country have the audacity to decide for another which city it can make its capital? Even Berlin remained in the possession of the Germans after they were defeated in World War II, although they deserved to lose it. Jerusalem has always been the capital of the Land of Israel, at least since King David purchased it.

In more modern times part of Jerusalem became controlled by the Jews after the War of Independence in 1948. In 1967 the rest of Jerusalem was returned to Jewish hands when Jordan tried to take the Jewish part and instead lost its own section, which included the Old City and the Kotel. It was a war that Israel did not want or start, but one which it won quickly and quite miraculously.

Classically, three of the justices on the US Supreme Court who voted against Israel were Jewish. What an "Erev Rav" type of thing to do! It has been pointed out by many throughout history that secular Jews in high gentile positions are not always something to be proud of, but rather something to be concerned about. This was a good case in point.

Essentially what their decision meant, at first, was that children born in Jerusalem would not be considered "Israeli" by American authorities. If they applied for and received American passports, Jerusalem would be listed as their place of birth, but not the State of Israel.

Although offensive, for Jews around the world this was really not a big deal, or so many thought at the time. Perhaps it should have been, though. Perhaps it should have been seen as a sign, a divine sign, indicating the direction the world was going at that time. After all, wasn't it the fulfillment of the following?

> Three times in the future Gog and Magog will war against the Jewish people and against Jerusalem (Mizmor 118:9). He will assemble there and anger the nations to go up to Jerusalem with him... (Drushei Olam HaTohu, Chelek 2, Drush 4, Anaf 12, Siman 10)

* * *

He was a zealot by nature, a zealot's zealot. He was one of those people who love God, Torah, and the Jewish nation so much that personal well-being comes second. You wonder how such people survive since they are always putting their necks on the line for one cause or another. Fear of the consequences often makes the rest us cower.

Not him though. When word of the decision to take Jerusalem away from the Jewish people reached his ears, he didn't waste a minute letting others know how he felt about it. Nor did he hold back on his plan for action, and also made it clear to those around him—Jerusalem is worth fighting for.

It took time before he made headlines. At first they were only local and for the most part went unnoticed. But when others began to echo his words and quote his opinions, politicians started to pay attention. Some were impressed by his opinions and resolve, while others were disgusted and angered. Some even called for his arrest just to shut him up. The fact that he wasn't breaking the law was completely unimportant to them.

Before the dawn of Facebook and Twitter, it would have taken a lot longer for people like him to catch international attention. Before the age of social media he might not have amounted to anything more than a local hero. Today, however, you can barely sneeze in public without ending up on YouTube. How much more so when you create a political storm as well.

Not being tech savvy, he had no idea of the impact he was having. He wouldn't have cared much even if he had. In his world all that mattered was whether or not Heaven was paying attention, and what God thought of his actions. As far as he was concerned, he only had to please his Creator, and that would take care of everything else.

He was right, perhaps in more ways than he cared to be.

* * *

"What do you have on him?" the senior CIA analyst asked his team of assistants.

There was silence as all five continued to scan their computers for something, anything, that might incriminate "him."

The team leader waited, beginning to sense that he wasn't going to be able to give the president what he wanted. And he hated not giving the president what he wanted. Everyone did.

"Come on, ladies and gentlemen," he said with a false air of formality, "there has to be something...a disgruntled employer...an angry girlfriend...an unhappy previous wife!"

Some smirked. Clearly their leader had no idea with whom they were dealing. People like him didn't have disgruntled employers, angry girlfriends, or previous wives. They belonged to another age, a simpler one of high morals and stable family life.

Smirking, though, could be at the cost of their job. The work was stressful but the challenge and technology were awesome. The pay was great too and so were the benefits. They got rid of their smiles as soon as they appeared.

"You have to give me something!" he barked. He was disgruntled and, loosening his tie to prepare for a longer haul, he added for impact, "I'm not the only one who will answer to a higher authority for failure!" He was right about that, but not about the Higher Authority to which he would eventually have to answer.

The only effect of his words was to make fast-moving fingers move even faster. As quickly as information came up on their screens, it was pushed away by newer data. But the CIA analysts, all high-caliber recruits, couldn't find anything worth exploiting to put an end to the activities of the Israeli activist. It was frustrating for people who usually have no problem finding dirt on a target of the US government. Frustrating and impressive.

"This guy is squeaky clean," one analyst finally admitted. It was a cliché that no one had heard for decades because it had stopped applying to just about everyone.

The team leader absorbed the words, and then spit them back out again in disbelief. "No one is squeaky clean," he said, "not these days." He added, half seriously, "We even have things on the Pope."

The analysts looked at each other, wondering

if it were true. With all the scandals currently rocking the Church, it seemed likely that it was.

Their leader's comment only made it more difficult for them to accept the fact that they couldn't break through and find something that would take the rabbi down. It made one of them wonder if this rabbi were really human.

* * *

"This guy…" the president began to say…

"Rabbi," he was corrected.

"This rabbi…" he began again, trying to sound as if he were not angered by the interruption and correction, although he was, "is becoming one very big headache."

"Tell us something we don't know," those assembled around him thought to themselves.

"I understand he was a virtual nobody at one point and only recently has become a political figure," the president said.

"He's not exactly a politician," one of the president's closest advisors explained. "He's more like…an activist."

"The whole Jerusalem issue," another close advisor added, "is his thing."

"He is completely against making Jerusalem an international city," the first one continued. With the president it was important to look as if you were on top of the job even if you weren't. "He claims that Jerusalem is the capital of Israel, always has been, and always will be."

"There are still American Indians who claim that Manhattan belongs to them," the president said, sarcastically, "but you don't see anyone giving it back to them."

That got a smile from people in the room, especially those visible to the president.

"He's not the only one," a voice said from the second row. "The problem," the voice continued, "is the support he is getting. If I didn't know better, I'd say that he is building a resistance movement against international policy, whether he knows it or not."

There were a few moments of silence as people considered the situation, some checking their notes.

"If you don't take him out of the picture," an ominous voice said from the back, "the problem will only get bigger, even out of hand."

The voice was easily recognizable, although not very likable. There was something sinister about it, but for some strange reason the person it belonged to had the president's ear. Being a civilian, he didn't even belong at such a high-level meeting, but the president wanted him there.

Ironically, although President Truman, also a Democrat, had a civilian for an advisor, his was in favor of the Jewish state, not against it.

No one spoke for a moment. Even if the voice were right, the others in the room felt that it should not dictate government policy, not that the current president was one for protocol.

"What do you suggest we do?" the president asked.

The man sighed, as if what he had to say next were difficult for him. It was not.

"War" was all he said.

"War?" the chief-of-staff said incredulously. "Against an American ally?" He paused and then added, "Are you out of your mind?"

A debate began. As the cabinet members argued among themselves, the president sat back and waited before green-lighting the idea. He first wanted to see the reaction of members of his support staff before revealing his plan. No one, except the person at the back who suggested it, knew that the whole thing had been a setup, planned beforehand.

In actuality the president, in his heart of hearts, had never considered Israel to be an ally, but rather a roadblock to a different world. Like the State Department, he felt that the formation of the Jewish state had been a mistake from the very beginning, although he paid lip service to its survival.

For years he had been looking for a pretext to cut Israel off. Part of his problem were the Jews living in the US. Although numbering only six million, they were a politically powerful group. This was the first issue he had to solve when dealing with the "Israel Problem."

Instigating riots in cities around the US, however, gave him a pretext to "protect" local Jewish populations in internment camps. Now some instigator, or rather rabbi, he facetiously corrected himself, was giving him an excuse to invade the Jewish state.

The pieces were falling into place, he thought, and he smiled to himself. If only he could have seen God's smile, he might have thought twice about his role in history. It was very biblical.

People, especially leaders, inevitably pay a price for their arrogance and narcissistic attitudes.

VERY LITTLE IS ever what it seems to be on the outside. Sometimes that's good, but sometimes it's very bad. That's why there is a mitzvah to judge a person on the side of merit, since what we see is rarely the whole story, or even part of it.

Who are Gog and Magog? The enemy. Who is Mashiach? The hero. But who are they really, on the inside, and not just on the outside? The body, after all, is simply a vehicle. It's like a "car" to get around in. It may be amazing in appearance, but at the end of the day, just as with respect to a car, it is the driver who makes the difference.

A veteran driver in an average car can often drive far better than an inexperienced driver in a more powerful car. Likewise, a great soul in a weak body can end up being far more powerful than a weak soul in a strong body. Brawn is a valuable asset but rarely more valuable than brains. Bodies are crucial but never more so than the souls that give them life, especially since the former die and the latter, in general, do not, allowing them to have an ongoing impact on history.

Equating "modern culture" with "biblical history" is considered paradoxical by many today. Once upon a time man was intellectually underdeveloped. A long time ago he was also spiritually unsophisticated. He didn't know much about how the world worked and, often victimized by it, he deified the forces of nature so that he could "bribe" them. This lame effort at climate control resulted in religion and eventually the Bible.

At least this is what many would have us believe. Agnostics and atheists trivialize religion and mock the service of God to justify doing whatever they feel like doing. It is a simple equation for them: No God, no religion, no Bible, and therefore, no moral obligations. Without absolute truth there is only subjective opinion, which can make life a lot more carefree. Hitler, ysv"z, pursued and murdered the Jews for this very reason.

The "good guys"? They are the people who agree with them. The "bad guys"? They're the ones who oppose them, and impose their idea of good upon others. Gog and Magog? A biblical myth. The Messiah? Any kind of savior who defends their version of good. He certainly doesn't have to be religious, or even Jewish. He only has to stand up for principles that their society holds dear.

It is easily agreed that the bodies of today are not the same as the bodies of people from "biblical" times. It is the souls that drive these bodies—which according to Kabbalah are far from new—that create controversy. Their mandates are not the same, even if their methods for carrying them out are.

Simply put, souls reincarnate. They come and they go, and then come and go again. A lot may change over time regarding the bodies they use, but each time the soul returns, its nature remains the same. Consequently, the soul can bring the world of the Bible into modern times, something the average person may not recognize without some biblical and kabbalistic background.

Just as the nature of the driver influences the "effect" of the car, the nature of the soul influences the "effect" of the body. An ancient Pharaoh-like soul can end up giving a modern body a Pharaoh-like look and effect, albeit clad in an expensive European suit. Likewise, a Moses-like soul can cause a modern-day body to have a Moses-like resemblance, albeit in a cheaper Israeli suit. Modern similarities to ancient figures are more than mere coincidence.

Such ideas can also help to explain historical anomalies. For example, why is it that some people try to rise in power and do everything necessary to achieve that goal, but only fail, while others seem to cheat the system and come out on top? Why do some people gravitate towards good while others seem to be pulled in the direction of evil?

Since historians tend to look for "natural" answers to such unnatural circumstances, the truth often eludes them. They focus on current political trends and historical circumstance to frame the events of the day, not even considering that other powers might be at work. Not believing in higher planes of reality, they cannot see how they themselves could be the cause of what is occurring and how it's occurring.

First there were the European leaders. One might have reasonably thought that after the Holocaust they would be repentant and would overcome their latent antisemitism. Instead, shamelessly, they created pretexts to attack the Jewish state. In true Amalekian fashion they focused more on undermining Israel than on dealing with the growing Arab problem around them. Although it was consuming them, that seemed to matter less than destroying everything Jewish.

Then there was the American leader himself. In quieter moments he might have questioned his motives for pushing the Jewish state to submit to UN proposals that clearly endangered its continued existence. Others did. He must have known, at least on some level, that his cause was not about right or wrong, but was based on a stronger affiliation to the Muslim world. Others knew.

What was driving him? Why was he so committed to a state for the Palestinians when he knew full well, as did everyone in his cabinet, that creating one would only result in a second Gaza? Those who voted for him, including many Jews, assumed that he knew something they did not, and trusted him. They were right about the first part, wrong about the second.

He had known all along that Iran had the bomb. He knew that the naysayers were right, that giving Iran nuclear leeway would be dangerous for the Jewish state. What people didn't realize was that although the man they saw on the outside was naively pursuing peace with Iran, his soul on the inside was intentionally loading a gun aimed at his Jewish nemesis.

When Naval HaCarmelli cursed King David, it says that "his heart smote him." Kabbalah explains that this means that he knew on some level that, being the reincarnation of evil sorcerer Bilaam, he was reincarnating to fix the sin of trying to curse the Jewish people back in Moses' time. Thus, although cursing King David may have felt right at the moment, it felt terribly wrong after he did it.

Likewise, the American leader felt emboldened. Only after setting the final war of Gog and Magog in motion would he finally sense the historical significance of his actions, when it would be too late to undo what he had done.

Mashiach was also beginning to sense that there was more to himself than he had noticed until then. As he was being prepared for his mission, he began to realize that there was more on his inside than the outside revealed. Humility, however, prevented him from reaching the logical conclusion.

Instead he just did what he had always done —the will of God—to the best of his knowledge and ability. In the past he had been compelled to respond to a crisis because it was his inherent nature to do so. His compulsion now to do what history was asking of him came from even deeper inside him.

He had never met or spoken to any of the world leaders who were planning his departure from the political stage, if not life altogether. He wasn't worthy or important enough in their eyes to deal with directly. Rabble-rousers rise up from the ranks of the underdogs and can easily be put down as fast as they ascend. The means to do so were easily available.

Ignoring the rabbi, however, made his job easier. He didn't have to waste time answering to anyone but God. It was the first of many tactical errors that Gog and Magog have always made. This time it would cost them their existence—forever.

* * *

The tanks moved into position. The Israeli Navy did also. It wasn't a good feeling to be so greatly outnumbered. Incredibly outnumbered. Israeli soldiers were good but not that good. Even with the air force flying above, they were greatly outgunned. They calculated that it would take less than a few hours to lose both the war and their beloved country. The end was near.

"This is going to be one incredible test of faith," one Israeli soldier said to another. The second soldier didn't even acknowledge his words.

"This is exactly what was predicted," he continued. "It says that in the final war it's going to look completely hopeless for the Jews...as if everything has failed...as if all were lost."

"All is lost," his friend deadpanned, continuing to look straight ahead at the future source of that loss. After a silence, the first soldier continued.

"Listen, I don't know what to tell you that will change your outlook. But we don't have a lot of time left to get it right."

"That much I agree with," the second soldier said, misconstruing the words of the first soldier. "I figure it will take about 30 minutes for them to run right over us."

"Ain't gonna happen," the first soldier said, with what seemed to his friend to be misplaced confidence.

"How can you be so sure?" the second soldier asked. "We're outgunned ten times over at least." He paused for a moment to further assess the situation. "All good things come to an end," he said with finality. "I guess our end has come a little quicker than I thought."

"Danny," the first soldier said, "you have to stop that. What's coming up is going to push our faith to the limits. I know you're not that religious..."

Danny laughed out loud at the understatement. He was as secular as they came.

"But you have to believe me," the first soldier continued. He paused before his next words. "This entire war, as crazy and militarily overwhelming as it is, will not come down to weapons. It will come down to faith in God. FAITH IN GOD," he emphasized, as much for himself as for his secular compatriot.

"Stay with me..." he continued. "Stay with God. Things will happen like never before and you have to be ready for that, otherwise..." His voice trailed off, uncertain of what to say next.

Danny looked into the eyes of his friend. "You really believe in this stuff, don't you?"

"Well, yeah, of course!"

Danny went back to observing the enemy, but for the first time he considered his friend's words. He wasn't sure why his heart was softening, but he suspected it might have to do with the seriousness of the situation or, more accurately, the hopelessness of the situation. If ever there were a time for him to believe, he thought to himself, it was now. He certainly had nothing to lose by doing so.

Danny looked back at his friend and said, rather awkwardly, "Okay. I'll believe."

The first soldier gave him a look that suggested he wasn't convinced. After all, no one changes that fast, not even in a foxhole. But when he met Danny's eyes, he saw something in them that for the first time made him think that maybe, just maybe, his fellow soldier was finally coming around.

"Now I know Mashiach is here," he said jokingly, as if to lighten the moment a bit. "Danny believes? Mashiach must be here!"

* * *

The prime minister surveyed the latest military intelligence. The situation was in fact hopeless. Although he had given the command to arm the nukes, he suspected that when push came to shove, he wouldn't use them. He was not a religious man per se, but he still worried about answering to God "later on."

* * *

The American leader, a.k.a. "Gog," also surveyed the latest intelligence. He was already planning how to deal with the defunct State of Israel after the war. It never occurred to him, not even for a minute, that within six hours— only six hours—he would be regretting his very existence.

* * *

"Allah has been kind to us," the Persian leader said to his general. "The Zionist enemy will be destroyed without our having to use a single weapon of our own!"

"Perhaps there will still be a need for them," the Iranian general said, relishing the idea of finally obliterating the Jewish state.

"Perhaps," he said, smiling to his military friend, when all of a sudden the smile vanished from his face. As the building they were in began to sway, the two men looked at each other, momentarily puzzled. Then their eyes widened as they simultaneously yelled, "Earthquake!" and ducked beneath the closest table.

Thousands of miles away Mashiach had merely lifted his arm. But he knew that it was having a dramatic impact on an evil enemy of the Jewish people in a faraway land. The end, indeed, was near, and was getting closer by the minute.

6

HaMashiach

SIRENS WERE SCREAMING everywhere. Air-raid sirens weren't yet sounding throughout Israel, but those too would start soon. These sirens told the pilots of the multi-national force to man their planes and prepare to take to the skies. Ships at sea were alerted to prepare for Phase 2. Someone high up had made the decision. The war was on.

The Israelis already knew what was happening. This was intentional, part of an intimidation tactic. It was intimidating all right, but it didn't stop the Israeli pilots from doing what was necessary to prepare for the battle of battles. The country had already been on red alert for days, but the sirens now blaring told everyone that the situation was about to become far more serious.

Hamas assumed that with Israel distracted by greater problems, it could act with impunity. Its own barrage of rockets were aimed as far north as they could reach, and numerous rockets began to fall. The Iron Dome went into action, successfully knocking out many of them high up, but the sheer quantity meant that some would make it through, endangering civilians.

The government had anticipated this. It knew that Hamas would use the opportunity to weaken Israeli forces, and prepared for it. Although in previous wars the IDF had acted with restraint, that was no longer possible. Nor did it make any difference in the eyes of the world. The Jewish people needed victory and they needed it quickly and decisively. Blanket bombing supported by tank fire and cluster bombs halted the attack, while tunnels were blown up with terrorists trapped inside. This forced Palestinian citizens to flee in all directions, while some waved white flags of surrender. Those who did so were shot by their own military.

It was a different story on the other borders. Israeli tanks stood their ground, but there were enemy tanks in all directions as far as the eye could see. IAF jets circled above, a small fraction of the number of enemy planes. No skill or technology could possibly level that playing field.

To their credit no Israeli soldiers showed

signs of panic. Israeli pilots and soldiers knew their fate, and were prepared to fight to the finish. They had no idea how long they would last, but suspected that it would not be long at all. Nevertheless they were prepared to die defending their beloved land, as others had done before them on many occasions.

Miles away, he could "feel" their courage. He felt two emotions simultaneously. He was proud of his people but sad for them as well. He knew that a happy ending was in store, but he also knew that they would be worrying about their future until the end. He knew their despair, and that it was part of the "filtering" process in advance of the Messianic Era. Not everyone was meant to survive.

When the enemy received the order to enter Israeli airspace, he turned his head in the direction of the enemy planes. He could not see them or hear them in the distance, but he could sense them. He "knew" what was happening and what was to happen, and he stopped walking. He waited.

A few seconds later he felt his right arm rising. He couldn't tell if he himself were doing it or if something else were in control, but he certainly was not going to resist. When his hand was higher than shoulder level, he imagined sending energy through his arm into his hand and then into the sky above, pointing in the direction of the imminent air attack.

Nothing actually came out of his hand. Nevertheless, he saw a rapid change in the sky in the direction his hand was pointing. Clouds began to develop overhead in what had been a cloudless sky, and the clouds began to swirl, expanding and gaining speed as they rotated. The circle kept getting bigger and bigger as it spread out in all directions.

"Red Leader One," the lead pilot of the UN Force heard in his helmet. "We're picking up a significant weather disturbance to the east. Can you confirm?"

Red Leader One looked to his left and was surprised to see what had been a perfectly clear desert sky suddenly become consumed by a massive, churning cloud.

"Copy that," he said into his built-in mic. "Advise."

"We're checking it out and will let you know momentarily," Command Center answered.

"Where did THAT come from?" Blue Leader One asked, a hint of concern in his voice.

"Out of nowhere!" Red Leader One answered as he slowed his jet down to subsonic speed.

"Look at the size of that thing!" Green Leader

One jumped in. "Back home in Idaho we'd call that the makings of a tornado."

Command Center cut in. "Red Leader One," the soldier at the controls said, "You are a go for mission."

Red Leader One was uneasy with the command but he didn't question it. It would never even enter his mind to do so. He was a soldier of the highest level of commitment and went wherever he was told, no matter how great the risk, no questions asked.

"Okay, boys," Red Leader One said to the others, "back in formation. This is a green light."

"Roger that," the squadron leaders answered, one after the other, as their onboard computers kicked in once again and set them up for what was to have been the first of many bombing raids on Israeli soil. They knew that the Israeli fighter pilots were some of the bravest and most talented anywhere, but they were hoping that the huge number of planes against them would compensate for that.

However, as the first squadron came closer to the Israeli border, the churning cloud suddenly expanded at an impossible rate. Within seconds sixty planes with the most advanced military technology imaginable were swallowed up and cut off from the rest of the world, literally. The radar screens just went blank.

"Red Leader One, Red Leader One, this is Command Center...do you copy?" the air traffic controller repeated with urgency. He tried the other pilots in the squadron as well but got the same response—nothing. A minute later the storm system moved on, but there was still no communication with the planes. There were no planes!

There was only silence at Command Center, except for the crackling of the radio in the background. The American general overseeing the operation was stunned. He had seen a lot of unusual things throughout his long military career, but never sixty warplanes vanishing into thin air. He didn't know what to think. He didn't know what to say.

"Are they still stuck inside that weather system?" a lower ranking officer incredulously asked. "Could it have dragged them along with it?"

The man at the controls was the first to answer. "Unlikely. It seems to be dissipating and there is still no sign of any aircraft."

"Is there anything on the ground?" The general asked, overwhelmed by what had happened.

"Satellite recon has found nothing so far."

"Where did those planes go?" the general asked himself, wondering whether the Israelis had some new technology that even he didn't know about. He immediately dismissed that idea. Should he risk sending a second squadron to the same fate?

Then his mind turned to the task of informing the higher-ups, but he didn't know what to tell them. "Get me the president," was all he could say.

* * *

"What do you mean, they are missing?" The Israel PM said to the general.

"Just what I said, missing!" he repeated.

"Where did they go?" a cabinet minister asked.

"If we knew," he said sarcastically, "they wouldn't be missing, would they?"

The prime minister absorbed the news. He was both elated and concerned. They had fended off the first attack without even firing a shot. On the other hand, what destructive force could not only take out the most technologically advanced military craft in the world, but do it in such a way that not one fragment remained. Did the planes just vanish into thin air?

Such an event was not something that could be kept secret for very long, on either side of the battle. As the story spread, it was also embellished, but the main point was not lost. Sixty warplanes were missing, "swallowed" by swirling clouds, and then completely disappearing. No one knew what to make of it.

Almost no one. Some Jews believed that Mashiach was already here and would win the war for them. This event only made them more certain that they were right.

In the meantime, with the first part of the job completed, still miles away from the battlefront, he began walking again in the direction of Jerusalem. Soon he would reach the back lines of the Egyptian forces poised at the southern Israeli border. As the Egyptians looked north for the enemy, destruction was in fact coming from the south.

7

V'aph-Al-Pi

"THEY ARE WHERE?" General "Iron-Fist" Borden screamed into his phone. It was a secure line, but not emotionally secure for the poor guy on the other end.

"Israel," he repeated, trying to sound unfazed by the verbal assault.

"How the..." As hard as it was, he held himself back from saying what he wanted to say, and continued, "How in the world did they get there?"

As different scenarios ran though his mind, including having to report to the high command, he asked, "Did they crash?"

"Not as far as we can see," was the response. "They're just sitting there...in the desert, just north of Be'er Sheva."

The general thought for a moment. War always throws you something new, but this was weird, and very costly.

"All the planes?" he questioned.

"As far as we can tell," was the answer.

"What about the pilots?" the general asked with concern. "Did they die? Did the Israelis pick them up?"

"It seems as if the cockpits are still closed. There are no Israelis there yet but you can bet they're on their way."

General Borden rubbed his forehead, completely unsure of what to do next. So he just continued with questions.

"What about communications?"

"We've tried all channels...no response to any of them so far."

All of a sudden the only rational explanation occurred to him, and he shuddered to think it. "Did they defect to the Israelis?"

There was a slight pause, not because the idea hadn't occurred to the man on the other side of the line, but because he had no good answer, and the general was all about good answers.

"Three full squadrons, General?" was all he said, throwing the ball back into the general's court.

"Besides," he volunteered, "these men are the

best of the best. It's highly unlikely that even one went to the other side, let alone three squadrons!"

The general had already thought of that before he asked the question. But he had a puzzle to solve and he had to first eliminate all the obvious possibilities. Defection was one of them.

* * *

"What?" the Israeli PM asked incredulously. "Sixty US fighter planes just showed up WHERE?"

"Ramon," the commander answered.

"You're sure?" the PM pressed.

"As sure as you are sitting in front of me," the commander confirmed.

The PM thought for a moment. "And the pilots?"

"Still inside," as far as we can tell, the officer said.

"Doing what?" the PM asked.

The commander looked at his fellow officers in the room, not sure of what to answer this time. "We don't know" was all he could say.

"You don't know?" the PM replied, this time incredulous at the lack of intel.

"We scanned the planes. As far as we can see, the planes are in good working order."

"Are they drones?" the PM asked, concerned.

"We detect human life on board."

The PM got up and went to look out the window of his office. Looking at the beautiful view from his office helped him think, and reminded him of what he was fighting for.

"Has anyone tried to communicate with the pilots?"

"No response," was the answer.

"Well, Commander," the PM said clearly confused and frustrated, "did anything else normal happen today?"

The officer smiled. "No, sir."

"Good!" the PM said sarcastically. "If anything interesting happens, you'll let me know, right?"

"Yes, sir!" the officer said as he stood up to leave. Had this been the Oval Office, the officer would have formally saluted before turning his back on POTUS. This was Jerusalem, however, and the Israeli leader neither expected such formality nor did he get it.

* * *

Red Leader One sat in his cockpit, wondering what to do next. As far as he could tell, his aircraft was in good working order. Only his communications system seemed to be down. He couldn't communicate with his home base or his wingmen. He couldn't talk to the Israelis even if he wanted to, which he definitely did not.

Soon he would have to anyhow. As he looked down the runway on which he was parked, he saw Israeli military vehicles racing his way. He saw half-tracks with soldiers and machine guns sticking out in all directions. He also saw tanks on both sides of the column. It occurred to him to unleash his payload at the oncoming and unwelcome troops, but a little voice inside told him that more likely than not it would cost him the planes and all his men. By the time he finished that thought, soldiers were already pointing their guns at the cockpit window. The scene was surreal. The entire episode was surreal.

How did they even get there in the first place?

Who landed the planes?

Why was there no damage?

The questions were good, but not ones that the Israelis could answer. They had the same questions and, like the American pilots, they had no answers either.

* * *

"That's ridiculous!" the MK said as took another sip of his coffee. "Sixty planes? Out of nowhere?" he asked his aide.

"Nowhere," the aide confirmed.

The MK considered how it could have happened. Did the government employ some new secret defense tactic, keeping him out of the loop? It wouldn't have been the first time, and he felt his blood boil at the thought.

"What are they saying about it?" he pushed, maintaining control.

"It depends on whom you ask," the aide answered, knowing that his boss was faking calmness. "Some are calling it defection...others are calling it some new secret weapon...and the rest are calling it..."

"Don't tell me," the MK said with a condescending tone, finishing, "They're calling it a miracle!"

The aide merely smiled.

"I hate that word!" the MK said with disgust. "Every time something happens in this country that people can't explain, they call it a miracle!" He paused to catch his breath. "There's no such thing," he said arrogantly.

The aide wasn't at all religious, but he had enough respect for those who were to refrain from commenting. "Maybe there's a God, maybe there isn't," he had often told himself. "But in any event I don't need to anger Him unnecessarily. I may not be religious, but I'm not stupid either," he would remind himself.

"Get General Goldman on the line!" the MK told his aide. "I want to find out what it is we're not being told."

"No problem," the aide said picking up the phone and dialing the general. He didn't expect to reach him at such a time, and he certainly didn't expect him to divulge top-secret information. But it was his job to try just the same.

* * *

He knew everything that was transpiring. He knew where the planes were and how they got there. He knew about the commotion it was creating on both sides of the border, and he found it amusing. He had changed so much, but some things hadn't changed.

He knew that there was an Egyptian patrol headed his way, and he could just about see it with his eyes. He already knew that they would mistake him for a Bedouin and suspect him of working with ISIS. He knew they were trigger-happy and had orders to "shoot first and ask questions later."

"You must be kidding!" one patrol officer said to his partner in Arabic.

There were at least two Egyptian battalions in

the area and reinforcements on their way, and they had to deal with a donkey driver? A nomad? He lifted his gun, getting ready to shoot. Why drive all that distance when they could solve the problem from where they were with machine-gun fire?

He wasn't worried. But they were. What was a Bedouin doing there anyway, in the middle of nowhere? And what was he carrying? A stick? And why was he pointing it at them? The one driving immediately slammed on the brakes and brought the jeep to a halt, causing the other to hit the dashboard. His Sig 552 Swiss-made gun flew out of his hands and out of the vehicle.

The driver immediately stood up on the seat and, aiming his gun in the direction of the donkey rider, pressed down on the trigger. The gun didn't fire. He quickly checked to see if the safety were off and what might have jammed. Convinced that everything was as it should be, he took aim and fired again.

This time the rapid-fire machine gun went off, exploding in the hands of its owner and killing his fellow passenger.

The "Bedouin" took note of what happened, thanked God for his safety, and continued on with his journey. There was a lot left to do and not much time to do it in. There were still three Egyptian battalions to pass through in order to get to the Jewish camp. He wondered what God had in mind for them.

* * *

CNN was the first to leak the story about the planes, but it didn't take much longer before all the major news stations were talking about it. Analyst after analyst, and anyone who might remotely have something to say about what happened, was interviewed. THIS was the fight of the century and, not necessarily believing that it was also the LAST one, they were only concerned about ratings.

After all, the war was taking place far from where they lived. The danger was quite distant from the ones they loved. Regular programming still went on with only infrequent interruptions for news. Everything was about to change, but who at the time knew it? Who at the time could have anticipated it?

Not the President of the United States, that's for sure. Nor the Prime Ministers of England, Germany, or Russia. As far as they were concerned, it was just a question of giving the green light for an all-out attack, and within hours the State of Israel would be no more. Local Jews would have to accept that reality or face imprisonment as enemies of the state. The world was looking brighter all the time.

"How did the Israelis do it?" the president asked calmly. Inside he was fuming. He definitely did not like it when things didn't go according to plan, according to HIS plan.

"We don't think they did," was the answer.

"Then who did?" the president followed up.

"We don't know," was the response.

"You don't know?" the president asked, feigning incredulity. "The CIA, the FBI, and all those pricey black-ops intelligence units can't figure out how sixty of the most sophisticated and, I might add, most expensive military aircraft in the skies on a raid show up at an Israeli air base somewhere in the south, unscratched, on the ground, and no one knows how it happened?"

The president leaned forward and, elbows on his desk, cupped his head in his hands. Then he rubbed the back of his neck vigorously, always a sign that he was very uptight, and said calmly, "Okay. Give the command to start Phase 2."

As military people quickly got up to get Phase 2 into action, the president added for good measure, "Let's just hope that the ships don't end up in some Israeli harbor until we send them there ourselves!"

Within seconds sirens went off across the entire Fifth Fleet. Battle stations were manned. Phase 2 was about to begin in order to quickly and decisively end what was intended to be the last Middle-East war.

As tank units rolled closer to the Israeli border, tightening the noose, the truce in Syria was holding up, as it was with ISIS elsewhere. Deals were made and souls were sold. Apparently the nuclear deal with Iran was just the beginning of a rash of crazy agreements that everyone seemed willing to make if the end result were the elimination of the Zionist state.

Sh'yitmamai'ah

"CIGARETTE?" HE SPOKE fluent English with a strong Israeli accent.

"No, thank you. Bad for your health," came the clearly sarcastic response.

"So is flying an F-16 at supersonic speeds," the Israeli said.

The American pilot smiled, bested. He chose not to respond further.

"Coffee?" the interrogator further asked, noticing that the pilot had not helped himself. "Or is that also bad for your health?"

The truth is that the American would have loved a cup of coffee and it would have been one of the first things he would have reached for after returning to base. But he was in Israel now, the land of the enemy, and how could he be sure that the coffee wasn't drugged?

Knowing exactly what the American was thinking, the Israeli picked up a cup for coffee. Saying nothing, so that the sound of coffee being poured would be clear to the pilot, he then helped himself to a muffin and sat down. The American studied his every move.

He took a sip of coffee, and then another, obviously enjoying himself. He took a bite of the muffin and, almost automatically, the pilot's mouth made a slight motion as if begging on its own for some food. He hadn't eaten for at least 12 hours.

"So," the Israeli said, looking at the name on the pilot's suit, "Captain Higgins…"

Cutting him off, the American said, "I'll take that coffee now."

The Israeli smiled politely. He got up, picked up a cup, and poured some coffee. "Milk, two sugars?" he asked.

"Fine," the pilot said. "Thank you," he added, reasoning that he could still afford to be polite, especially since he had not yet been mistreated by the Israelis.

"I'm going to ask you a question," the Israeli said, "that you have probably been asking yourself for the last couple of hours."

The pilot smiled.

"How did you end up in Israel, you and your entire squadron...without a single radar picking up any of you?"

The pilot looked down at his coffee, and then up at his interrogator, and smiled. The Israeli returned the smile. Neither one said anything for a few minutes.

"I know you have been trained to tell the enemy your name, rank, and serial number. And you know that now I'm only asking politely, but we have methods of extracting such information from you without even laying a finger on you," he said, studying the American's facial features for the slightest bit of revelation. "And of course," he added for impact, "we have truth serum, to make sure we get the real story."

Looking straight into the eyes of the man across the table, the pilot simply said, "Colonel John Higgins. US Air Force. Serial number 18602701." He said nothing more, as he reached for his coffee. The Israeli smiled at him and, getting up from the table, said, "It is a pleasure to meet you, Colonel Higgins. My associate will be with you shortly to administer the requisite drugs." He walked across the room, thinking his work there was finished, and reached for the handle to make his way to the next pilot on the list.

"I don't know," the pilot blurted out. He calculated that it might be better to speak while conscious, controlling the flow of intel, than to do so under the influence of some serum that could force him to divulge a lot more than he might need to."

The interrogator stopped in his tracks, turned around, and said, "You don't know what?"

"I don't know how we got here, how we ended up on your runway, and why nothing happened to our planes."

"You don't know anything about that?" he asked, sitting down once again.

"Nothing."

"Sixty F-16s just hopped the border and landed south of Be'er Sheva, and no one has any idea how it happened?"

"We thought you did it."

The Israeli studied the pilot's face and body movements again, as he was trained to do. He was looking for signs of a person who is lying, or at least holding back the truth. He saw none.

"You mean like a tractor beam?" the questioner said, taunting him a bit.

The pilot looked up. "Yeah, well, kind of." Realizing that sounded stupid, he added, "I don't know what you used, but maybe it works the same way."

The Israeli shook his head and smiled. "Colonel," he said, "we can barely shoot you out of the sky at supersonic speeds, let alone snatch your planes at such speeds and land them without even a scratch!" He paused as he considered what to say next, and then added, "And without anyone knowing, either!"

Now it is was the American who studied the face of his interrogator for the truth. Did the Israelis have a new secret defense system, and was this just a charade to hide it? He suspected the answer was yes, but the strain on the face of his questioner seemed to imply otherwise.

If the Israelis weren't responsible, the American wondered to himself, then who was?

If the Americans weren't responsible, the Israeli wondered to himself, then who was?

It was going to be a long day, especially since each pilot would more or less say the same thing. In time they would get all the answers, but by then it would be too late to do anything about it.

* * *

"They do not like to use the word 'miracle' at all" the elderly rabbi said. "A miracle implies God, and God implies morality. They don't like morality."

The man sitting with him on the bench smiled while looking out at the spectacular view in front of him. He was the same age as the rabbi, but his life had been very different from the venerable sage's. Once upon a time they were study partners, but at age 18 they had gone in different directions. He himself took the path of a future successful businessman while his study partner took the path of a future Torah leader.

But they had remained friends, close friends. They even learned together on occasion, and the man was careful to send checks on a regular basis to his friend's yeshivah. The bond between them was deep.

"Do you blame them?" he asked his friend. "Between what they feed them through the media and the onslaught on materialism, it's hard to be moral today."

"Hard, but not impossible," the rabbi said. "It's all about self-integrity. A person has to love truth more than himself."

"They've been told that there is no truth today."

The rabbi paused for a moment, and then explained, "The soul knows that there is truth."

"Ah," the businessman said," but they do not believe they have a soul!"

The rabbi smiled. "Then they will be very surprised when they find out that they were wrong, and very disappointed, I might add, that they didn't find out sooner."

His friend also smiled. It was not the answer

he had expected from the rabbi. He didn't argue, as he often did, but moved on.

"What do you think happened to those planes?" he asked, pretty much knowing the answer already.

"I think what you really mean to ask," the rabbi said, "is 'What does it mean?'"

"What can it mean?"

The rabbi turned to look at the businessman, who was already facing him. They looked into each other's eyes.

"It means," my friend, "that we have arrived."

"Arrived? Where?"

"There."

"There where?"

"'There where,' the rabbi repeated, mocking his friend. "I think you already know what I mean!"

The man inhaled deep and slowly. "You think this is it?" he asked cautiously. He knew that his friend longed for Messiah to come, but he himself never made predictions nor took those of others seriously.

This time the rabbi took the deep breath. "Yes," was all he said.

"Yes?" his friend asked, astonished. "How can you know?" Then he added playfully, "You haven't been speaking to him, have you?"

The rabbi smiled.

The smile dropped from his friend's face at the same time, "Wait a second," he said half seriously, "you're not him, are you?"

This time it was the rabbi who lost his smile. "Would I be sitting here and chatting with you on a park bench if I were?"

"Hey," his friend protested jokingly. "I need saving too!"

The rabbi smiled once again. Then he became serious. "It says in the Zohar that when the Final Redemption is close at hand, even school children will be able to predict it. Well, that's all they do these days."

"That's your proof?" the man asked, somewhat disappointed.

The rabbi looked into the eyes of his friend and said, "Yes. And no. The Zohar is the Zohar and kids often repeat what they hear at home. My proof," he said for emphasis, "is all the strange things that have been happening recently."

"Strange as in miraculous?" he asked the rabbi.

"Yes," he answered, "strange as in miraculous."

The man opened his mouth to say something but what came out instead was a siren. Well, at least that's the way it seemed because as he intended to speak, an air-raid siren went off rather loudly. They both looked up and saw the siren mounted on a roof across from the park.

Automatically they got up to run. They were in Jerusalem and had about two minutes to get to the nearest air-raid shelter in safety. As they ran, the businessman looked back, although he didn't know why, and he saw a large white explosion. And then another. And another after that. The explosions kept coming one after the other and he no longer noticed the people running and screaming all around him. He just found himself coming to a halt and standing in wonder.

The rabbi, realizing that his friend was no longer with him, turned to call him to catch up. He was surprised to see him stationary, staring up at the sky. Then he saw why, and he too stopped and stared. Soon just about everyone who had been running for shelter also stopped and watched the spectacle.

At first the man had been impressed with the success rate of the Iron Dome. But looking back, he saw something altogether different. The clear blue sky had all of a sudden become cloudy, and the clouds had merged. Even more amazing was how missiles entered the cloud but didn't come out. Explosions could be heard and bursts of light could be seen, but nothing came out the other side of the cloud!

Moments later, the man turned to find his friend, the rabbi, who was looking at him. The rabbi was too far away to actually hear what the man was saying, but he was able to read his lips: "He's here."

The rabbi nodded his head ever so slightly.

*   *   *

If the rabbi and his friend thought that they were the only ones astonished by what was happening, aside from the people around them, they were wrong. Through his binoculars the admiral could see what the radar specialists in the belly of his ship were watching on their screens. When the expressions of shock subsided, there was only silence.

"What the..." was all Admiral Jorgenson could say. He was fifth-generation navy, and not particularly religious, but he still remembered enough from Sunday School to recall the story of the Cloud of Glory that had swallowed up the arrows of the Egyptians to protect the fleeing Jewish people. He also remembered his father telling him that it was all a bunch of, well, you know, myth.

"Just a myth," he whispered to himself as he once again looked through his binoculars.

"Hold your fire!" he called out, and the command was echoed throughout the entire fleet. He simply did not know what to do next, or what the cause of the spectacle was. Planes had gone missing and then mysteriously showed up on enemy soil. Computer-guided missiles couldn't penetrate the air space of the enemy country.

"Still surveying the situation in the distance, the admiral asked the officer next to him. "Explanation?"

The officer could only shake his head in sympathetic disbelief. "I have no idea, sir."

* * *

This time the Israeli Prime Minister did not stay and ask for an explanation. What was the point? Instead he excused himself, which raised eyebrows from those around him, and headed for a private room. Locking the door behind him, he sat down at the desk, uncomfortable about making the call. He made it anyhow.

The phone rang only once. "Yes?" was all the other side said, as if the person were expecting the call.

"I need to speak to the rav," the PM said with a sense of urgency.

Without even asking who it was, the voice on the other side of the line said, "He knows. He's been expecting your call."

"Shalom," the rav said softly, "before asking

about the well-being of the PM, who responded politely before saying, "I need some answers quickly."

There was an audible pause. Over the wire the prime minister could hear the older man breathing.

"Your place or mine," the rav asked.

"I can be there in 15 minutes," the PM said. "But no one can see."

"No one will see," the rav said, before hanging up the receiver. Turning to his assistant, he said, "We have some preparations to make. We need to work quickly."

* * *

The president sat there, stony-faced, stoic. The news was not good. Strange things were happening. Lots of good questions with no good answers. But he was too committed to back down. Instead, his resolve just increased. Maybe the Israelis did have technology they hadn't shared. They were a clever bunch, he gave them credit for that. But he had more firepower, a lot more firepower.

9

Im-Kol-Zeh

"I REALLY BELIEVED we were right. I really thought that Israel was the evil empire. I was so ashamed to be Jewish!"

These words came from someone who the previous year had joined an organization created to oppose the Jewish state. While some called for a boycott of Israeli products only from "disputed" areas or lands, this group called for a boycott of everything Israeli. It tirelessly fought long and hard for divestment and sanctions against Israel, and had gained a lot of support along the way, both political and financial. The members felt extremely self-righteous, especially since they too were Jewish.

This raises a question: How many times

throughout history have Jews turned against their own? The kapos did to their own what even some Germans wouldn't do to the Jews in their charge. There had been Jews in earlier times who tortured their own brothers on behalf of the Church. Now Jews were prepared to throw their own people under the bus once again.

Like those before them, they thought it would earn them special status among the Gentiles. They believed their willingness to betray their own people would prove how loyal they were to their host nation. Like those before them, they refused to learn a lesson from history: Once a Jew, always a Jew, at least as far as antisemites are concerned.

This is likely because, as they fail to realize, antisemitism is not simple racism. It may look like racism and act like it to some degree, but it goes beyond racism. Sometimes it affects even the most assimilated and unrecognizable Jews, people who considered themselves to be more Greek than the Greeks, more Roman than the Romans, more German than the Germans, and more American than the Americans.

Not knowing Torah and not understanding the roots of antisemitism, they assumed that it results, like other forms of racism, from differences. So if it hurts when you do something, don't do it. Assimilate. Integrate. Turn against your own people when the rest of the world does.

Antisemitism is not simply racism. It is supernatural. It is divinely sent, especially when few differences seem to exist between the Jewish people and the gentile nations. It comes to make a Jew more recognizable, and it has done so throughout history.

The truth hurts, however, when you are on the other side of it, and they were clearly on the other side of it. They were also stuck in internment camps, mistrusted by their gentile "hosts" and disgusting to their Jewish brothers and sisters. It was now clear who the enemy was and the enemy obviously wasn't Israel. Even worse, they had spent enormous amounts of time, money, and energy on helping the enemy against their own people. Pride turned to shame, security to fear. Even if they survived, where could they go?

"Erev Rav," one said to the other, shaking his head in disbelief.

"What?" his associate said.

"Erev Rav. That guy, the Jew in the cell we passed on the way in, called me 'Erev Rav.'"

"What's that?"

"I may not know much about Judaism, but that term I know. It means 'mixed multitude.'"

"Mixed what?" the associate asked.

"The mixed multitude. You know, the Egyptians

who left Egypt with the Jewish people." Seeing that his friend still wasn't getting it, he continued, "Didn't they teach you anything in Sunday School?"

"I skipped that," his associate said. "I'm not into fiction, especially religious fiction."

He smiled wryly. He too hadn't believed the stories in the Bible, learning from an early age that the Bible was written by men and enforced by men. All of a sudden he no longer felt so comfortable with that point of view, and he wasn't sure why. He continued anyhow.

"The Erev Rav, supposedly," he added, so that he wouldn't completely lose credibility with the only friend he had at the time, "were the ones who always caused problems for the Jews in the desert...If I'm not mistaken, they even built the golden calf."

"What golden calf?" his associate asked, clueless.

"Wow, you really don't know anything Jewish, do you?" he said, surprised. "Didn't your parents ever show you the movie "The Ten Commandments"?

"Bro," he defended himself, "I'm 25 years old. That film was probably watched by cavemen!"

He smiled, and this time it was his associate who continued the conversation. "Besides, what's the connection anyhow?"

"It's not a nice one."

"You're kidding me," his associate interjected sarcastically, as he continued, "They see people like you and me as doing the same thing they did?"

The associate was unfazed by the supposed insult. He had been called worse things by others who didn't agree with his line of work. His own father had called him a "traitor" and a "danger to the Jewish people," so why should he care if some stranger compared him to fictitious characters in an ancient book? "So," he continued, "like I said, what's the connection?"

He thought for a moment. He was surprised to see how a little time and a lot of perspective could so radically change his point of view. How could he have been so blind?

"You still don't get it?" he said.

"Not really. I mean," the associate went on, "just because you're Jewish doesn't mean that you have to agree with everything other Jews do, does it? The Israelis were doing bad stuff, and we were trying to stop it."

"Were they really?" he said, surprising even himself. "Did we ever thoroughly check out the situation...I mean see it from the Israeli point of view?"

The associate gave him a strange look, as if perhaps he were losing his mind and taking the part of the enemy, rather than the ally.

"We saw the contradictions, but we didn't want to pay attention to them. We also saw the world ganging up on Israel and we joined in."

"Now you're going to the other extreme," the associate complained. "The Israelis were guilty of many things!"

"But maybe not as many as we thought. Maybe...maybe..." his voice trailed off as he became absorbed in the thought that he might actually be the self-hating Jew his brother accused him of being.

There was a pause, but the silence said more than words. It expressed regret more sincerely than speech could have done. The two of them stared into space, confused, lost, and disconnected.

All of a sudden they heard a commotion. When they could not make out what was being said, they moved closer to the door.

"What's he saying?" the associated asked.

Squinting, as if it made listening easier, all he could make out was something about...the Messiah being here. "Great," he thought to himself, "People are losing their..."

Before he could finish his thought, the door to

their cell opened, revealing two large MPs. "Come with us," they said in a stern voice.

* * *

They say the transition to the Messianic Era will be very difficult for some. So difficult, in fact, that the shock of it may kill them. After all, to have bought into the idea that there is no God, or that Torah is not His word, and then to find out that the opposite is true...

It's similar to the story of Joseph and his brothers. When he finally revealed himself to them, they were speechless. It would have been amazing enough had he just survived after being sold into slavery, but second-in-command over Egypt? That was so outside the box that they almost died when they found out the truth.

Granted, some people just didn't know better. But for those who could have and chose not to, it was a different story. Besides, it's a different world today. Today over the internet you can learn almost everything about anything in the comfort and privacy of your own home.

Technology is a double-edged sword for another reason as well. Before we had much of it, even the weather was mystical. Believing in miracles was a lot easier then. In our rush to understand how every little thing works in order to better control our world, we became dependent on logic as a means of explaining just about everything.

In fact people have become so addicted to the "scientific" approach that when something occurs that cannot be explained by science, it's almost as if it doesn't really exist. For some, the word "miracle" isn't even part of their vocabulary.

So however amazing it was that several $1.5 million state-of-the-art cruise missiles entered a mysterious cloud and never came out again, it doesn't necessarily mean that something supernatural happened. "It just means," the deniers insisted, "that the Israelis have some kind of hitherto unknown tactical advantage that they had kept from their allies." If what happened is sufficiently analyzed, surely it can be figured out and overcome.

* * *

The president slammed his fist on the desk, something he had rarely done during two terms in office, at least not in full view. He was known for being tough, but not angry. Everyone knew he got angry, but they also knew he had the ability to keep public displays of it in check. The current situation apparently had pierced his armor.

"How can they have such a weapon without our knowing about it?" the American leader asked in a threatening tone of voice.

There was silence. No one had an answer.

Looking directly at the CIA director, he said, "We have intel on what the prime minister of India eats for breakfast, and we don't know anything about a cloud-making device that eats million-dollar missiles for dessert?"

The director squirmed in his seat. He had fought in just about every war the Americans had been in over the past 30 years, and had seen things that most people could never stomach. Still, very little intimidated him more than criticism from his commander-in-chief.

"We have reached out to every contact we have over there. They all say they never heard about such a capability. Either this is one of the best-kept military secrets of all time," he added, "or…"

"Or what?" the president interrupted.

The director paused for a moment. On one hand, he felt compelled to say what he had planned to say next but, on the other hand, doing so was antithetical to his entire mode of operation. Vagaries were the last thing he was supposed to supply.

"Or…" he said, as part of him urged him not to

continue with the rest of the sentence. With 30 men and women hanging on his words, he was compelled to continue. "Or it is something else."

All eyes shifted to the president for his reaction.

"Something else?" the president intoned.

The director said nothing more. He wasn't going to dig his hole any deeper than he already had.

"Something else...as in..." the president began, prompting the director to be more specific, but the head of the Central Intelligence Agency, for the first time, had nothing to add.

When no answer was forthcoming, the president sat back in his chair. He wanted to put his feet on the desk, which he often did in private, but it didn't seem appropriate at the moment. So he crossed his legs and, addressing the entire group, said, "Ladies and gentlemen, in case anyone hasn't yet seen the memo, we are at war. And, I might add, it is a war that involves about 30 countries that look to the United States of America to lead them to victory, quick victory..."

Before the president could finish his soliloquy, someone's phone went off. The president automatically turned in the direction of the beep, just as another phone went off, and then another. When the phone on his own desk rang, he picked it up immediately, hoping it was good news for a change.

It wasn't.

* * *

The prime minister declined a cup of coffee. He had come for information and he needed it quickly. He wasn't a religious man, but he knew enough to have respect for the elderly rabbi, the kabbalist sitting before him.

"The answer is yes," the rabbi said, eliminating all preamble.

"What was the question?" the PM asked, caught off guard.

The rabbi smiled warmly, and the PM had the impression that he had some hidden knowledge.

"You have come to find out if what has happened is a nes—a miracle," the rabbi said, sipping his tea.

The PM thought for a moment. That was not the question he had in mind. Then he thought some more and realized that it really was the question he had come to ask.

"A nes?" the PM asked.

"Let's not waste any more time," the rabbi said forthrightly. "You have much to do and little time. It is really very simple," he continued, as he got up and slowly walked toward the window. His movement revealed his age, or so he mistakenly thought. He walked like a man in his 70s, but he was actually in his 90s.

"Mashiach is here, this is the War of Gog and Magog, and history as we know it is coming to an end, and quickly," he said, looking out the window.

The statement hit the Israeli PM like a ton of bricks. His first thought was that the rabbi had finally lost it, and that his imagination was doing the talking. His second guess was that he was losing his marbles. He didn't know what to say next.

"You're not saying anything because there is nothing to say," the venerable sage told the Israeli leader. "But you are wondering what to do now," he added, turning around and looking into the PM's eyes. The PM was at least 10 meters away, but he felt the gaze of the rabbi penetrate his soul. He felt exposed.

"Teshuvah," the rabbi said in an undertone. "You have to do teshuvah—repentance, and everyone else around you as well." He paused to think, and then added, "The whole world needs to do teshuvah. The Almighty is judging us as we speak, and surviving means doing teshuvah, and quickly."

As the prime minister sped back to his office, he heard the rabbi's words in his head over and over again. How was he going to present the rabbi's message to his cabinet...to the people? Should he even try?

As he pondered his predicament and the strange events that had been occurring, an idea came to him, from where he had no idea. Suddenly, he found himself instructing his driver to take him to a local television station. He immediately jotted down some notes about what to say.

* * *

In the distance, he smiled. He saw it all and was pleased with the direction everything was going.

10
Achakay

"THERE ARE UNCONFIRMED reports that the Allied Forces are about to begin an all-out invasion of the Jewish state," the CNN correspondent said. "Apparently limited efforts to intimidate the Israeli government to withdraw from areas inside the Green Line have thus far failed, and the UN has given the green light for an all-out invasion."

"Many are questioning the wisdom of such a military operation, given Israel's reputed nuclear stockpile. Am I correct, Dr. Ford?"

The man sitting next to him, who had been waiting patiently for the cue to speak his mind to millions of viewers, suddenly looked into the camera to answer the question. On the screen below him was a banner that read "Professor Dr.

William Ford: Expert on Middle-East Affairs."

After the usual time delay between question and answer, the "expert" spoke. "That's right, Bill," the professor confirmed. "You have to wonder what Israel will do when its back is up against a wall. Everyone knows that a cat is the most dangerous when it is cornered, and the Jewish state is definitely cornered."

"Professor," correspondent Bill Whithers continued, "I guess the big question on everyone's mind is whether Israel has nuclear capability and, if it does, whether it will use it against the attacking forces."

"I don't think it's a question any more of whether or not the Israelis have the bomb," the Professor said. "I think it is safe, or perhaps safest, to assume that they do...and many of them." Dr. Ford paused to allow his words to be absorbed by millions of viewers. "As to whether or not they will use them as a last resort," he added, "again, I think it would be safest to assume that they probably will." Looking straight into the lens he said, "I mean, who wouldn't? The Americans have, and the Russians certainly would in a similar predicament."

"Especially," Whithers stepped in, "since the Jewish state is no stranger to genocide. If anyone is paranoid about being destroyed, it has to be the

Jews!"

"Well, that's true," the Professor agreed. "The only thing I would say is that over the years I have gotten the impression that even when push comes to shove, the Israelis still might not use their bombs."

The correspondent sharing the screen with the professor unconsciously gave a look that seemed to express his surprise at such a statement. "Why not?" he asked, almost more personally than officially. "Given their track record of what they call 'self-defense,' it would seem likely that they would do whatever they must to survive."

The professor gave a small smile that suggested that he was going to say something ironic. "Because," he began, "they have a tough time doing things like that."

"Even though," Whithers said, somewhat argumentatively, "others would not think twice before using the bomb on them? Iran has sworn that it will one day blow the Jewish state off the face of the earth!"

"Well, that's the ironic thing," the professor said, "even though the media and the Arab world have vilified the Jewish state and made it out to be the bad guy, it's not so true."

Whithers' face dropped slightly. He had not

expected the discussion to go in this direction. He had not been the one to suggest the interview, but now he had to do his best to control the dialogue. The last thing the station wanted was a pro-Israel interview.

"Professor, I'm sure you've seen the countless photographs depicting Israeli brutality…"

"Actually," the professor interjected, "I was there on several occasions when they were taken."

Whithers thought—rather hoped—that the professor was back on track, but was prepared to cut the interview short if necessary.

"According to what I saw," the professor continued quickly, sensing Whithers' frustration, "the Israelis were provoked for the shots, sometimes even by the cameramen themselves. The Palestinians seem to know a good photo op when they get one…"

Oops. Whithers gave his tech guy a look to cut the interview, but at that moment he happened to be on the phone. This gave the professor time for a few more sentences.

"I'll tell you something else, Bill," the professor pushed forward, as Whithers did his best to look as if he weren't squirming inside. "I think the UN is making a grave mistake…and the people behind the UN's decision to go in…"

At that moment the screen went blank.

Both Whithers and the professor thought that the network had pulled the plug. But from the way people were running around, it seemed to suggest that the network had nothing to do with it. Something else had happened, and no one knew what.

All of a sudden the power went out. Complete darkness was everywhere. People freaked out when the back-up generator failed to kick in. No one knew what to do.

Just as someone yelled out, "EMP ATTACK!" the power went back on, and people began to breathe once again. Within seconds phones started ringing and beepers went off. News poured in. Something big had happened in the interval. But what was it?

"WHAT?" a very excited and animated station chief yelled out. "Was it nuclear?"

Suddenly the question Whithers had asked the professor went from being academic to actual. A nuclear war had just started, and that could not be good for the world.

* * *

It was understandable that people would think it had been a nuclear explosion. The flash was brilliant and the shock waves could be felt for miles around as the ground split and entire tank divisions fell into the abyss. Just like that.

But there was no signature mushroom cloud. Professionals looked through binoculars, they looked from satellites, and they listened to first-hand reports, but no signs of a mushroom cloud, only of tremendous damage. The experts were again baffled. There was confusion all the way to the top, on both sides of the border.

The Israeli tank commander thought he had gone blind. Not expecting a nuclear explosion, he had been watching the enemy from miles away when the flash went off, and the shock waves rocked his tank. He was thrown back against its side before falling several feet to the floor of the armored vehicle. It took him a few minutes to re-gain consciousness.

When he did, he heard the tank driver calling out in a panicky voice, "Colonel Dagan! Colonel Dagan!" while administering ammonia inhalants, otherwise known as smelling salts.

Opening his eyes slowly and trying to figure out where he was, he asked, "What happened?"

For a moment he thought they were all dead. He knew that a nuclear blast at such close range should have melted the tank and everyone inside. The smell meant that either they had died and gone to hell, or that they were still alive, not a much better scenario at the time. They certainly hadn't gone to heaven.

"No idea," the driver said. "Couldn't have been nuclear because we're still here. At least I think we are."

The colonel slowly lifted himself to his feet, clearly in pain, so the driver helped him. On one hand he was afraid to look beyond the inside of his tank shell, but on the other hand he knew he had to. He had to know what happened, and if the enemy were about to overrun them.

It was impossible to see out the window. Whatever combusted had sent something clear across their stretch of desert, something that scorched their windows.

"Who wants to go up top?" he asked rhetorically, putting one hand on the ladder as he prepared to ascend.

Getting the lid of the tank open was another story. The heat must have melted it shut, he thought to himself, not a good sign. There are stories of soldiers getting stuck inside their tanks, which became tombs. He did not want to die in a tank.

"It's stuck," he shouted. "Get me something to open it with."

A few seconds later a soldier handed him a large metal bar. The colonel pounded on the lid as hard as he could, but it didn't seem to help. Then, as if in response, he heard knocking from the out-side. Unsure if someone were there or if it were just some debris flying around, he knocked again, and again the response was more knocking from the other side of the lid. The only question now was whether it was from friend or foe.

The question was quickly answered. "Colonel Dagan?" a muffled voice asked in Hebrew.

As he looked at the other men in the tank, he wondered if the enemy knew who he was and which tank he commanded. The others seemed suspicious too.

Fortunately there was protocol for such situa-tions. Through the metal door the colonel yelled, "It is hot in Eilat at this time of year," which would only make sense to someone who knew the code. He waited for the response.

"But it is cold in the Golan," came the muffled reply from above.

He got that one right, the men thought to themselves, looking at each other. But they took out their pistols just in case.

"Cold, yes," the colonel continued in Hebrew, "but damp enough for grapes to grow to make wine."

They tensely waited for the response.

"Red wine," came the voice from outside the tank, "but not white wine—Cabernet, not Merlot."

The colonel smiled at his men. That was the entire code, totally correct. Looking back up towards the lid of the tank he yelled up, "Can you get us out?"

"We're trying," came the response. "Try pushing from inside."

It took 20 minutes and a lot of banging, but together they were finally able to pry the lid open. Fresh air poured into the tank, and the men inside breathed deeply, grateful that it was their own who had rescued them.

One by one they climbed out of the metal box on tracks and, looking in the direction of the blast, Colonel Dagan asked, "What was it? Nuclear?"

"We don't think so," the young corporal said. He must have been all of 21 years old, but he carried himself like someone with years of military experience. "No radiation and no cloud."

Looking through his binoculars, the colonel said incredulously, "And no tanks…"

He scanned what was previously the enemy line for any sign of movement, but there was none.

"Where did they all go?" he asked the young corporal.

"As far as we can tell," Corporal Goldman answered, "down."

"Down?" the colonel asked.

"Down," the corporal confirmed.

"Into the ground?" he asked looking away from his glasses and at the corporal.

"Into the ground," he repeated.

Dagan looked back through his binoculars into the distance, searching for clues. He asked, "How?"

"We don't know," the corporal answered. "There was a huge flash. It was followed by an enormous shock wave which almost turned our vehicle over. The next thing we knew, they were gone, as far as we could see."

As he listened, the colonel saw some movement, but not the kind he was looking for. Trying to focus perfectly, he said, "What the…"

Goldman reached for his own binoculars and looked in the same direction as the colonel. Seeing the same image, he asked matter-of-factly, "Bedouin?"

As the two officers scrutinized the figure in the distance, too far to really make out clearly, a jeep raced in. It came to a quick stop, and officers jumped out and ran in the direction of the two men.

After a quick salute, one officer asked, "Colonel Dagan?"

"Yes," the colonel answered back.

"We need you to come with us, sir," the officer said motioning toward the jeep.

"What about my men?" the colonel asked.

"Other transportation is right behind us to pick up survivors."

"Survivors?" the colonel asked. "Were there casualties?" he said concerned.

"Not as far we know, sir," the one driving the jeep answered. "But we need you to come with us immediately!"

"What's going on?" the colonel pressed.

The two officers from the jeep looked at each other, as if deciding whether or not to reveal a secret. The first officer said only, "Sir, we need to leave now."

Turning back toward his men and nodding to let them know they'd be okay, the colonel followed the two officers and got into the jeep. As they sped away, he thought to himself, "Wouldn't a chopper have been quicker?" Then out of the blue it hit him.

The image in the distance?

A man on a donkey.

A man on a donkey?

He shook involuntarily as shivers went up and down his spine. It was a distant childhood memory, but it was so vivid, he could have heard it yesterday. Although his grandfather had died long ago, not everything he told the future Israeli colonel-to-be was forgotten.

He felt a terrible dread in the pit of his stomach. As his body moved up and down in synch with the bumpy road, he unconsciously looked heavenward.

IT ALWAYS AMAZED him how something so small could be so deadly. It was just a pistol but, aimed at the right place, it could take a life in a single moment. He knew exactly where to fire.

Three times he had raised the gun to his head and three times he had lowered it. He was losing credibility in his own eyes, even as he knew that he could not go on. He loved his wife, he loved his children, and until recently he had loved his job. But all of a sudden, being leader of a left-wing anti-Charedi party didn't seem like such a noble idea.

He got the idea to do away with himself from a friend and colleague who had already done so, and for the same reason. The official report was that his friend had died in a car accident. He knew differently.

He was lost in thought when he heard the voice of his wife through the door. He was sitting in his study with the door locked and, after unsuccessfully trying the handle, she called to him through the door.

"Jacob?" She waited for an answer. "Jacob?" she repeated.

He could hear the nervousness in her voice. She suspected something. He tried to sound calm and in control, but it is hard to sound as if it's business as usual when you're about to take your life. He betrayed himself instead.

"Please don't," she pleaded with her husband of 27 years, in a soft, unsteady voice. She felt terrified and helpless.

He said nothing. He didn't know what to say.

"Whatever it is that is bothering you," she said, "we can work it out...together. I just beg you not to do it."

Again, he said nothing. He looked down at the weapon in his hand and regretted not having used it sooner. Doing the deed with his wife within earshot made it very much harder.

"Think of the children," she reminded him, "and what it will do to them...They love you so much...It will torture them for the rest of their lives."

He knew that and had considered it. "Desperate times, desperate measures," he told himself.

Surprisingly, he felt more cowardly than heroic. As he thought some more, he heard a fierce banging on the door, which caught him totally by surprise. He wondered how his wife could bang so loudly, but then he heard a voice that was clearly not hers. It wasn't even a woman's voice.

"Jacob," a stern male voice said, "Open the door. It's Ariel."

As instructed by her brother-in-law, she had bought time. She engaged her husband in conversation to give his brother enough time to get to the house and save him.

"Ariel?" he thought, surprised to hear his voice.

His younger brother had betrayed the family. After the last Gaza war Ariel had turned his back on his extremely secular life, and therefore on his family, and had gone off to become a religious Jew. What others called military success, Ariel called miracle, and a reason to take a second look at Torah Judaism.

A year later, Ariel was Orthodox. It affected a lot of people but none as much as his older brother, Jacob. "In some respects," Jacob used to complain to his wife, "what Ariel did is worse than joining the Palestinians and fighting against Israel!" He decided to sever all communication with the "traitor."

"How did Ariel know?" Jacob thought.

His wife had told him. When she saw her husband becoming depressed, she became worried about him. When he locked himself in his study and would not come out, she texted her brother-in-law, who immediately came running. Now he was at the door and banging to come in.

"Jacob," I know what you are doing, and why.

Jacob looked down as the weapon, which seemed more evil by the moment. "Ariel had been right all along," he admitted to himself, "And now, even though I turned my back on him, he's here to save my life."

It only made him feel more desperate.

"You know I cannot go on," Jacob finally said to his brother through the door. "You know I built my entire life on the idea that there is no God."

"So that gives you the right to face Him earlier?" Ariel asked, half seriously.

Jacob smiled at the irony, but he no longer knew what else to do.

He felt trapped.

As he sat there, lost in his emotions, there was a loud noise. Ariel had broken down the door. It startled him, and the gun fired.

His wife screamed.

The kids came running.

Ariel approached his brother.

Although the gun wasn't pointed directly at the door, the bullet almost hit Ariel, missing him by only a few inches. "Great," Ariel said. "I survived the streets of Gaza but was almost killed by my own brother in his suburban home."

In the meantime his wife ran to him without even thinking about the gun in his hand. There was no danger anyhow, since he had only put in a single bullet, but she didn't know that. One bullet should have been enough, but he hadn't anticipated his brother breaking down the door and causing the misfire. He couldn't even kill himself properly, he thought wryly.

"Jacob," Ariel said, putting his hand on his older brother's shoulder, "we can fix this. People have done far worse and still made up for it."

Jacob looked up at his brother, saying nothing. He hadn't seen him for years, and he had aged. But looking into his brother's eyes, he saw a wisdom that, for the first time ever, he envied.

*　*　*

"Five, four, three, two...one!"

When the Israeli Prime Minister saw the blinking red light he knew that he was facing millions of viewers. He couldn't see any of them but they could all see him. Even leaders of others countries were watching him now and, thanks to social media, whatever he said would instantly travel throughout the world.

"What I am about to say," the prime minister began, looking straight into the camera, is and will sound, well, strange to many."

As the Israeli leader paused to collect his thoughts, the President of the United States, an ocean away, watched intently. He had developed a real dislike for the Israeli Prime Minister, and seeing him on the screen took away his appetite for lunch.

"You may be aware that recently American warplanes, part of an international coalition under the guidance of the United Nations, were sent to attack Israeli targets."

He paused as if waiting for acknowledgment.

"You may also know," the PM continued, "that they did not reach their intended targets, but were 'captured' instead."

The president growled to himself, but hoped that at least he would now find out how it was done.

"What you may not know," the PM said, "was that Israeli forces did not shoot down these planes nor did they escort them to an Israeli airbase."

The secretary of state looked at the president, whose eyes were glued to the screen in front of him.

"How did the planes end up on Israeli soil?" the PM asked, as if on behalf of viewers around the globe. As countless people sat on the edge of their chair to hear the answer, the prime minister disappointed them by saying in a humble tone, "We don't know."

"He's telling the truth," someone in the room for that very purpose said. "His facial movement...his voice...he's not hiding anything."

"Or he's just a very good liar," the American leader said. It was clear to everyone in the Oval Office except himself that he was in denial.

Although he could hear nothing, even with the earpiece he was wearing, the PM imagined millions of people around the world asking, "You don't know how sixty state-of-the-art American warplanes ended up on Israeli soil without a single gunshot? How is that possible?"

"All I can say at this time is that the matter is being investigated. It should be made clear, however," the PM emphasized, "that neither the IDF nor the IAF had anything to do with the capture and landing of the planes in question. Even the pilots themselves," he added for good measure, "have been questioned and are as shocked as we are about what happened."

Now there was a certain awkwardness about the prime minister, as if he were about to say something he did not want to say. Thousands of miles away the analyst squinted his eyes, detecting something else, something indefinable, in the face of his boss's adversary before him on a large wall screen.

"The other incident of which you are aware is the so-called cloud pillar. To my knowledge, this is not a freak weather system."

The PM paused for a moment before continuing, finding it difficult to accept the reality of what he was about to say, had to say.

"Even if it were, I have been assured, it would not have had the capacity to destroy missiles without destroying everything else around them at the same time. This is also being investigated as we speak."

"Truth again," the analyst begrudgingly admitted. This time the president looked at him, and noticed others around the room looking at one another in disbelief.

"As of this moment there are search teams looking for fragments of the downed missiles, but so far nothing has been reported or found."

The analyst didn't even bother to confirm the truth of that statement.

For the first time the PM looked away from the camera, down at his folded hands on the table before him. He was gathering courage for the part he had dreaded. Looking back up again, he began the "unusual" part of his speech.

No one knew what the Israeli leader was going to say, including his aides, which made them uncommonly nervous. The generals sat together in another location, uncomfortable about what their commander-in-chief would admit to the world on international television. They already felt extremely stupid for not knowing what happened to the planes and missiles.

* * *

He smiled from miles away. He was pleased to see that the Jewish leader was finally acting more, well, Jewish. They had never met, and perhaps they never would. He hadn't thought about the role a secular leader might play at the End-of-Days, and he was pleased to see that it was a positive one. He wondered just how positive.

As he approached the city limit, still on his donkey and arousing curiosity, there was one man in particular who caught his attention. As the elderly kabbalist approached the man on the animal, he became overwhelmed with sensations.

Coming closer, he felt a wellspring of emotion force its way to the surface, and he began to cry. Reaching the man, he took his hand in his own and said words he had waited his entire life to say, "My master, my teacher." Then he let go, stepped back, and said the three blessings that Jews have anticipated saying for generations. Slowly, deliberately, emotionally, and with eyes closed he said, "Blessed are you..."

*   *   *

In all his years in office the Israeli Prime Minister had never once quoted a verse from the Bible. In secular Israeli politics you quickly learn to keep religious beliefs private. Now, many years later and for the first time he felt the need to break protocol.

"The prophet Isaiah once said..." he began.

"What?" millions of shocked viewers thought to themselves. Everyone heard what he said, most knew to whom he referred, but no one understood why.

The Israeli general picked up the phone. It was a direct line so there was no need for identification. "What's he doing?" the general asked the person on the other end, concerned.

"I honestly don't know," the other said in an

anxious voice.

The PM stared into the camera and paused to collect his thoughts. It would be the last speech of his political career, of that he was sure. He had no idea how history would remember him, if at all. Somehow that didn't seem to matter to him any more.

"If he gets weird, cut the broadcast," the general said.

"I'm a step ahead of you," the voice confirmed.

"As a young boy," the PM began, "my grandfather told me about a time such as the one we are now experiencing."

"CUT IT!" the general shouted into the receiver.

"Done," the voice said calmly. However, before either could breathe normally again, they were surprised and angered to see the broadcast continue.

"My grandfather was not a deeply religion man," the prime minister continued, "but he remembered enough from the yeshivot of Europe to know that one day in the future history, at least as we know it, would reach its end."

"Why is he still on?" the general demanded.

"We suddenly lost communication with the station," the other voice said.

"Cut the power to the station!" the general yelled.

"We tried that too. Technical problems."

"Unbelievable!" the general said. "Get someone over there now and drag him away if you have to!"

"THAT would not look good on international television!" the other person shot back. "But I'll send my men."

The general slammed down the receiver. He turned towards the image of his leader once again and scrutinized his face on the screen, as if doing so might stop the PM in his tracks. It seemed to have the reverse effect.

The PM sat back in his chair. He felt unusually relaxed, unusually inspired.

"My grandfather told me about a time that the nations of the world would turn against Israel and try to eliminate the Jewish state. He said that our weapons, no matter how powerful, would not be able to save us."

"So why not just give up and back away?" a cabinet member asked under his breath, just loud enough for the president to hear.

"It scared me at the time," the PM admitted. "But then I grew up," he said. "I became educated, even attended Western universities. Over the years I 'learned' that the Bible was not divine and that my grandfather's tradition was more fairy tale than truth." He looked down, as if ashamed, as he said, "He died knowing that I rejected everything he had fought so hard to preserve."

Black sedans were minutes away from the studio. Miles away the generals waited to hear that the prime minister had been silenced.

"Like so many of my peers, not once did I question my educators about their beliefs. Never did we take the time to find out why our ancestors had believed so ferociously in Torah, and its many laws and customs. We just assumed, like all the 'intelligent' people around us, that man has gotten smarter over time. What they once believed, we agreed with each other, was out of ignorance and necessity."

At that very moment Shabak agents burst through the door with instructions to pull the plug and grab the prime minister.

They froze in their tracks. The studio was empty. The signal was false, a diversion. In anticipation, the prime minister had gone to a secret location to broadcast his message.

"HE WHAT?" the general screamed. "FIND HIM, NOW!" he demanded. "I don't care if you use every agent we have!"

The Israeli prime minister had become so caught up in his thoughts that he forgot he was actually addressing what became tens of millions of viewers, if not more. Simultaneous translation meant all nationalities could pick up the broadcast locally.

"How do we know for sure," the PM seemed to ask himself, but was really asking the world, "that there is no God, and that He did not once talk to man...that He did not once, a long time ago, give Torah to the Jewish people? How do we know for sure?"

The general sunk into his chair. He command-ed one of the most sophisticated armies in the world, but at that moment he felt completely helpless. If he couldn't stop his own prime minis-ter from committing political suicide, he thought to himself sarcastically, how could he stop a mas-sive enemy from destroying his tiny country?

"We don't know for sure," that leader said softly with a tone of humility. "We just assumed that we were right, just as we are assuming at this time that the miracles of the last few days have techni-cal explanations."

He intensified his gaze as if he could look through the lens of the camera and directly into the eyes of all the viewers. That was certainly the way it felt at the viewers' end.

"They do not!" he said, involuntarily hitting the table with his fist. "What has been happening cannot be explained by natural means nor do I think that we have seen the last of such miracles. There will be more miracles," he said confidently, "and bigger ones. And the Jewish people will not only survive," he said forcefully, "but we will be redeemed in a way that we have never been before!"

The television crew were stunned. They could not believe that their nation's leader was spewing political heresy. They didn't know what to do next.

"What you do from this point onward," the PM began to conclude, knowing his moments were numbered, "will be your own personal decision. It has to be."

Then reaching into his pocket and producing a small black knitted yarmulke, he said, "I for one have decided to once again believe the words of my grandfather who, although he knew much less than me, was far wiser than I could ever be."

The prime minister put the yarmulke on his head. Then, leaning forward onto the table and again folding his hands, he ended by saying, "Thank you for your time. It has been a pleasure serving you. May the God of Israel, of Abraham, Isaac, and Jacob, protect us all and save us from the plans of our enemies."

The screen went blank. There was silence in the studio as the prime minister and everyone around him considered what had just occurred. "Well, that went well," the prime minister said matter-of-factly. Then turning to the people around him he added, "Thank you for your help.

But now you really should be on your way. You can assume that this studio will be under siege in moments."

The crew looked at each other and, without saying a word, agreed to remain where they were, with their leader.

THERE WERE THREE types of reaction to the Israeli prime minister's speech: mockery, confusion, and commitment. When an international leader goes public in this day and age, claiming that God is behind the events of recent history, the arrogant mock. They are so sure of themselves and their level of intelligence that they cannot entertain the possibility that, as smart as they are, they might be mistaken, very mistaken. How can people with half their intelligence be right about something so obviously wrong?

Less arrogant disbelievers became confused. "What changed our leader's mind?" they wondered. "Was it that he lost his, or does he know something we do not, see something we can't see?

What should we think? What should we believe? Can so many smart people be so wrong about something so important? It's too confusing."

The third group did whatever they could, as fast as they could, to backtrack and express their willingness to do what God wanted. "If the prime minister, a smart and reasonable person, says that God is making things happen," they said, "then we are not the ones to disagree."

This was exactly what Heaven wanted. The only reason events were progressing as slowly as they were was to push people to take a final stand, make a final decision about where they were holding with respect to God and Torah. God is 100 percent fair, which means that it is up to us to take responsibility for what we choose to think or do. In a sense we are our own judges, and we determine and are held accountable for what we choose to do and who we choose to be.

This was the message that he came to deliver. If ever there were a moment of truth since the Jewish people accepted the Torah at Mt. Sinai, it was now. If only people would understand that.

* * *

As he stood there with the Western Wall behind him, he spoke to a single camera. A small crowd had formed around him, attracting the attention of others. Few, however, did anything more than take a quick look and continue on their way.

He began. "For thousands of years people have lived in the world as if it belonged to them, using it to satisfy their own personal needs and desires. As they lived from day to day, the only meaning they found in life was to survive and, when possible, physically thrive. Materialism has driven mankind for millennia. Few have focused on the needs of the soul."

One of the great accomplishments of modern technology is the way so much can be accomplished with so little. One small video camera belonging to an amateur newsman was filming the greatest historical event in recent times, and it was being picked up by large stations around the world. Within moments millions upon millions of people were watching him speak, including the President of the United States and other major world leaders.

"Who is this crackpot?" the American leader asked the people watching the broadcast with him in the Oval Office.

"We're tracking him now," CIA Director Furmer said.

"How could this be making international news?" Secretary of State Berry asked in a condescending tone.

"No idea," the CIA chief said. "All the networks just picked it up."

The voice from the Western Wall Plaza continued.

"What I am about to say will be comforting to some, disturbing to others."

The president sat back in his chair and crossed his arms in unconscious defiance. So did the British leader at 10 Downing Street and others in their respective offices around the globe.

"History as you have known it," he said. "is about to end."

"Yours too," a sarcastic voice said from the back of the Oval Office.

"How do I know?" he said, smiling knowingly into the camera. "I know because I have come today in the name of God, the God of Abraham, the God of Isaac, and the God of Jacob."

The number of people who cringed at that point, many of whom were Jewish by birth although Gentile by lifestyle, was known only to God. But it was a lot. He smiled again, as if he knew that as well.

"I have been told to tell the world that the time has come to make a choice, your final choice."

He paused, as if waiting for additional information.

"Why are we watching this lunatic?" the secretary of state asked, turning to look at his boss, surprised to see that the president was transfixed.

"Why is anyone giving this guy the time of day?" another voice asked.

At that moment, the FBI chief got off the phone. He had been talking to the director of CNN and was surprised to find out that the station had not chosen to pick up the broadcast. It had been hacked, forced to carry the interview, or whatever it was. Homeland Security was already on it.

It wasn't just CNN that had been hijacked, but all the news stations around the world as well. "Whoever this guy is," the head of Homeland Security said, "he's got a very sophisticated understanding of computer networks!"

The crowd in the meantime had swelled around him. Now people held phones in the air to take their own videos. Images of the man were bouncing around the world.

"Know that God is merciful," he continued, oblivious to the attention, "and He has waited thousands of years for the truth to become known and for Creation to fulfill its purpose. But mankind by itself came no closer to this today than it has come up to now."

Scanning the crowd before him, he added, "Over three millennia ago God spoke to the Jewish people..."

"Can't someone shut this guy up!" the head of a very large Israeli corporation yelled angrily. "He's a total embarrassment to the country! No wonder they want to run us off the face of the earth!" Turning to one of the managers in the room, he ordered, "Either change the station or shut the thing off. I don't care which, just as long as you get rid of this crazy person."

Changing the station accomplished nothing. Every channel showed the same thing, so the employee tried to turn off the television. It didn't respond. After fiddling with the remote control, he turned to his boss and said, "It doesn't seem to want to shut off."

The owner of the business became so frustrated that he picked up a chair in order to smash the television with it. He was only 56 years old and in relatively good shape but, as he lifted the chair, his face turned green. He dropped the chair and fell on its legs. Within moments a medic was in the room trying to revive him.

It took three electrical shocks with the paddles before the man's heart began beating again, albeit weakly. With an oxygen mask over his mouth and nose, unable to speak, he was taken on a stretcher to a local hospital.

The remaining people in the room, somewhat

in shock, took a few minutes to collect themselves. Finally one man picked up the upside-down chair and returned it to its place at the large boardroom table. Spooked, no one said anything. They just resumed their places around the television and continued to watch the broadcast.

The message in every language was the same: Decide. With 24 hours the world would undergo a major transformation and survival was a matter of belief. False beliefs would die and the people who held them would die with them.

"God is real!" he exclaimed. "The Torah is true, the only truth!" he said with emphasis. "Embrace it, and you will survive. Reject it, on any level, and you will not."

* * *

Not too far away and alone in her apartment, she was watching the man speak with every fiber in her body. She had survived World War II and every Israeli war since then. She had lost much family along the way but she had never lost her faith, not in God, not in the Torah, and not in redemption. Frail and in her late 90s, the only thing she questioned was whether or not she would live to see it happen.

As she watched, old, wrinkled, and dried up,

she was surprised to feel tears welling up in her eyes. She hadn't thought that, after all the crying she had done over the years, she had any tears left. Spilling out from her tired eyes, they rolled down her cheeks. She thought she would die then and there from the sheer excitement of the moment.

This time she did not reach for either her prayer book or Book of Psalms, both of which showed signs of fervent use. She simply looked heavenward and said in a soft and humble voice, "Thank you, Almighty, for letting me live to see this day...to witness Your redemption." She paused, thought for a moment, and then added, "Now I am ready to go."

If she could have looked into Heaven, she would have seen angels smiling. They had watched her for years, energized by her unbreakable faith in God and His Torah, impressed by how spiritually strong she had remained despite her many ordeals. She was a simple woman, known by few but cherished by her Creator.

"By tomorrow at this time," she heard the man on her old television say, "truth alone will reign forevermore."

Instantly, the broadcast ended. All the networks around the world regained control over their stations, still not knowing how they had lost it in the first place.

As the leaders of the Western countries weighed their options, the man at the "Wall" greeted well-wishers. Many stood back, unsure of what to make of this individual, dressed in what could only be described as biblical clothing, and of his message. Others rushed to take his hand and kiss it. Elderly people cried with joy while younger ones danced with happiness. The Messiah was among them and the Final Redemption was at hand.

The Jerusalem police looked on with both curiosity and anxiety. They didn't know what to make of the person before them, and they studied his every move. Some wanted to arrest him just in case, some purely out of hatred. If they hadn't worried about starting a riot, they would probably have dragged the right-wing religious fanatic away by his sidelocks.

Thousands of miles away world leaders spoke with each other and their cabinets. There were private calls and conference calls as the clock ticked. They didn't want to take the guy seriously but, given the strange events that had recently occurred, they felt obliged to at least talk about it.

Some countries did more than just talk. Some went so far as to pull out of the UN's war against Israel. But some others, who remained part of the international coalition, decided that they would not wait for the 24 hours to end. They would attack now, and with everything they had. He had known they would.

THE LINE BETWEEN arrogance and sheer stupidity is not always clear cut. That's because they are often the same thing. There is also much of both, on all sides of the line.

There were those who just could not accept the idea that when you attack the Jewish people, you attack God. Even after the recent events. Even many Jews couldn't accept it, some of whom were religious. How much more so secular Jews.

Then there were those for whom it just didn't make a difference. They chose to believe that no matter what the world might throw at Israel, the country could deflect it. They believed that the Israelis were so smart and so tech savvy that they would always be one step ahead of everyone else.

"If what the Israeli government allows us to know is impressive," they boasted, "just imagine how impressed we'd be if it showed us what we're not allowed to know!" Talk about blind faith.

The truth is that as smart and as capable as the Israelis were, they had their limits. As miraculous as their success to date had been, that too had its limits. Contrary to popular Jewish belief, which is really hope, there is a scenario in which Israel loses, and it seemed to be rapidly unfolding. Jews around the world, but especially in Israel, weren't waking up from a nightmare. They were waking up TO one.

A little humility goes a long way; a lot of humility goes even further.

As the world zoomed in on the upcoming destruction of the Jewish state, some people didn't bother to wait for it to actually happen. They were already toasting a brave new world without the Jewish nuisance. It never occurred to most of them that Hitler had done the same thing just over half a century earlier.

"They had their chance to make peace with the Palestinians," they rationalized to one another. "They chose to be stubborn. They have this coming to them." They felt completely self-righteous.

The Arabs and the Iranians laughed all the way to the bank. How could the world be so ignorant and gullible, they wondered. Were they dreaming, or was the destruction of the Jewish nemesis taking place without the slightest involvement on their part?

They had never stopped hating Israel. They would have destroyed Israel on their own at the first possible opportunity. Amazingly, Israel's own allies were now doing the dirty work for them. It could only be the work of Allah, they gloated.

The humble thought differently. It was a sucker play, they argued. God, the Jewish God, was setting up the people of the world for the grand finale, drawing them in through their own arrogance and ignorance. It might look as if God had abandoned the Jewish people and given their enemies a free ticket to do with them as they pleased, they warned, but that was only the way it looked. He may be a sleeping giant, but attacking His people is sure to wake Him up.

Religious rhetoric. That's what others called it. It might have worked on simpler minds hundreds of years ago, but not today. God had been kicked out of society—the US Supreme Court had seen to that. Unlike the people who built the first tower, modern man had succeeded in banishing God from the world, and was now the boss to do with it as he pleased. This time the new world order would take place.

* * *

The afternoon prayer service had finished. There were so many in attendance that people were squeezed into the hallways and balconies. The rabbi of the shul had offered his chair next to the holy ark to the man for whom the Jewish people had waited thousands of years. He humbly declined, however, and instead prayed right in front of the ark.

"I have never, ever, prayed in a congregation like this!" Michael commented to his friend Eliezer.

"No kidding," his friend responded while watching every move the man at the front of the sanctuary was making.

"What do you think they're talking about?" Michael asked, seeing some of the greatest rabbis of the generation surrounding and talking to the man.

"I can only guess," Eliezer said, "but I'd give anything to be a fly on the podium right now."

"Right," Michael teased. "You already bug enough people!"

"Ha, ha…" Eliezer replied. Getting serious, he then asked, "Do you know what this means…if he's really here?"

Michael smiled. He was 28 years old, married, and the father of three young children. His own father had passed away years ago, and his mother was in her late 80s and still living on her own. He had eight siblings, four brothers and four sisters, all of whom he got along with more or less.

His life was good but not spectacular. He had trained himself long ago to be happy with his portion. He had learned early, being the fifth of nine children, that jealousy helps no one and hurts everyone. His father, an only child, hated sibling rivalry and made sure at every opportunity that his children appreciated each another.

The downside of such a normal life of Torah learning and mitzvah performance was that he never imagined what it would be like if the Messiah and redemption came during his lifetime. Sure, he had often spoken about both, just like the next religious guy, but it never really touched his heart. Intellectually he believed in the idea of redemption and the Messiah, but emotionally...

"Are those tears I see in your eyes?" Eliezer asked, surprised by his friend's reaction. Even during his most difficult moments, he had rarely seen his friend show emotion. He couldn't remember if he had even seen him cry over the loss of his father.

"I guess so..." Michael said, pulling a tissue from his pocket. Blowing his nose, he asked his friend, "What do you think that was about? I don't even know where those tears came from!"

"I think you were answering my question," Eliezer said, "Apparently, you do know what it means if he is really…really…"

"Messiah?" Michael helped him out.

Eliezer smiled, on the outside and on the inside too.

*   *   *

"As we stand here right now, the nations of the world are moving into position for the final battle," he told the rabbis around him, whose faces betrayed the seriousness of the situation.

"Our people will be tested like never before," he explained. "Even good people will be frightened, and those with faith and trust will be pushed to their limits."

"What can we do?" a rabbi in his 90s asked.

"Everyone must be told, even those who will not listen," he continued to explain, "that this is a critical test. The people must know that no matter how dire the situation looks, how hopeless it seems, God is with us and will redeem us. Even if the enemy appears to be victorious, the people must remain steadfast in their faith in God."

"That will be very hard for many," another rabbi lamented.

"Will it be like in Egypt?" a much younger rabbi asked.

The man paused and smiled. "Very much so," he answered. "There are some things that still need to be rectified. The situation has become more difficult, as it did in Egypt, in order to speed up the Final Redemption. The people must know this and be encouraged to stay strong in their faith. If they make an effort, God will help them with everything else."

Before anyone could ask another question, the man became momentarily distracted, as if listening to something no one else could hear. Then snapping back to attention, he simply said, "It is time. I must go."

He turned around and faced the door. All of a sudden, like the splitting of the sea, people moved to the sides to clear a path for him. The man smiled, acknowledging them. As he walked, hands reached out from all over to shake his. When he reached the door, he heard a gentle sobbing.

He stopped for a moment and turned in the direction of the crying. As the crowd parted, he saw an elderly man, bent over, using a cane for support. He could barely straighten up and didn't notice that someone was approaching.

The man walked over to the old man and tenderly put his hand on his shoulder. Knowing that he spoke only Yiddish, he said to him softly, "He has seen your suffering. He knows the strength of your faith. He has not forgotten you. You have waited, and you will be rewarded."

Those in the room who understood Yiddish felt tears well up in their eyes. The old man, his hand shaking, feebly took the hand of the one speaking and kissed it. He blessed God for the good news, and the man for sharing it with him.

He gently removed his hand and turned towards the door to complete his mission.

* * *

All the pieces were in place. Tanks were lined up along the entire border of Israel. The Egyptians and Iranians were in the south. Russian commanders and advisors oversaw all the units. American, British, and French divisions were interspersed with Jordanian and Iraqi troops. To the north were the Syrians and Hezbollah, with smaller units from other countries around the world, including Japan. It was truly an international effort.

In the water, in the Suez, there were American and French ships, along with some Iranian vessels. It was a feather in the American president's cap that he had managed to bring Iran on side, making it into an ally. Then again, it wasn't hard for him to do, even at the cost of the old ally, the only democratic one in the region. How much convincing did Iran need once money started flowing back into its coffers with few demands?

Enemy ships also filled the Mediterranean, with all guns pointed at Israel. All that remained was for the order to be given, and an all-out 360-degree attack on the tiny Jewish state would be launched. An hour or two later almost nothing would be left standing. A nuclear bomb would be totally superfluous because the barrage of conventional warfare would accomplish the same goal, without radiation. It might even leave a few buildings intact for the conquerors to use once they started rebuilding the Jewish state as an Arab one.

If ever the power of a single command were felt, it was now. The president, in consultation with other world leaders, only had to say, "Go," or "Now," and world history would change dramatically and forever. A single word and an entire nation would be destroyed, and the world would be better off for it.

"What a solution," he thought to himself, "what a fi-" He caught himself. The phrase had never popped into his mind before and, now that it did, it triggered something inside him. But it didn't stop him. It only made him realize why Hitler was so bent on destroying the Jews of his time.

"Mr. President?" the secretary of state said, his hand over the mouthpiece of the secure line.

Looking up, as stately as he could be, the president knew what he wanted to hear. "Give the order," was all he said.

So God did.

The president had been right. His command would change the world, dramatically and forever, but not the way he envisioned. And he would certainly be remembered, but just not the way he had planned.

*   *   *

They all felt relieved, although cowardly as well. They had left Israel and, in many cases, family and friends in their time of greatest need. But what could they do? What could they change? Why should they pay with their lives for the mistakes of others? What point was there in being just another dead Jew? They had long ago voted to give in to the demands of the Arabs and their backers. They had warned of a deteriorating relationship between Israel and America, but it fell on deaf ears. It wasn't their price to pay.

The promise of relocation and a second

chance at life proved too enticing for them. The opportunity to become American, British, or even French, without ties to anything else seemed…liberating. They accepted that they would be riddled with guilt at first. It was only natural. It was only human. It was only Jewish.

Yet in all their running and escaping, it never occurred to them that more than they were leaving the Land of Israel, the Land of Israel was sending them away. They thought that they were rejecting the Land, but it was actually the Land that was rejecting them. They had divorced themselves from its history and its meaning, so they were sent away to foreign lands to confront their fate.

The gun was pointed.

It was about to go off.

Just not in the direction they had thought.

hyavo

THE WARS OF GOG and Magog had been predicted long ago, all three of them. According to the Talmud, it seems as if the first one were the potentially epic battle between the overwhelming large and well-equipped forces of the Assyrian King Sancheriv and the greatly outnumbered and outgunned Jewish forces of King Hezekiah.

Although the major battle was just hours from happening and the subjugation of the Jewish people hours from becoming reality, all had been miraculously avoided when a plague ravaged the ranks of the foreign threat during the night. Hezekiah had been sleeping soundly, which was an act of faith in God's redemption. Sennacherib was forced to flee in fear and disgrace, and was later assassinated while worshipping his gods.

The great and venerable sage Rabbi Israel Meir Kagan (1889-1933), the Chofetz Chaim, did not count that potential War of Gog and Magog as an actual one. Perhaps what disqualified it was the fact that the war was averted. The Talmud says that God wanted to make Sennacherib into Gog and Magog and Hezekiah into Mashiach, but never did.

The Chofetz Chaim died in 1933, just as Adolf Hitler became chancellor of Germany. Although he had only lived to see World War I, which he considered to be the first War of Gog and Magog, he correctly predicted World War II, which he said would be the second War of Gog and Magog, more devastating than the first. Unlike WW I, the Second World War, according to Hitler, was specifically a war against the Jews.

As for the third one...it was already taking place. If the Chofetz Chaim were watching it, it was from above with the rest of the angels. They were all there, at least all the important ones—the angels, that is. More than any other battle in the history of mankind, this one was a universal war that involved good and evil forces, both above and below.

Everybody was involved in this one. This was the war to end all wars because it was the war to end all evil, which was certainly not about to go down without a fight. If the Sitra Achra[1] were going to go down, you could be sure that it was going to take down as many others with it as it could. Divine Providence would give it the chance.

There is a Midrash that says that right before the Final Redemption the Jewish people will undergo their most difficult test of all. It says that the "Bnei Keturah," descendants of Hagar and Avraham, including the Arabs, will challenge the Jewish people. They will suggest that both the Jews and the Arabs offer a sacrifice to God to prove once and for all who His true people really are. If a fire comes down from heaven and burns up the Jewish sacrifice, the deal goes, then the Arabs will convert to Judaism. If the opposite happens, however, then the Jews have to agree to convert to Islam.

Confident that God would accept their sacrifice and reject the one offered by the Bnei Keturah, the Jews will agree. However, says the Midrash, things will not proceed as planned by the Jews. Rather, to their utter shock and confusion, fire will descend from heaven and will consume the sacrifice of the Bnei Keturah, not that of the Jews!

---

[1] Literally the other side, the opposite of holiness.

Consequently, the Midrash continues, many Jews will lose all hope and actually convert to Islam as promised. Only a small group will refuse and instead flee to the desert to save their lives and their faith. It will only be after this peculiar episode that Mashiach Ben David will finally come to lead the remaining band of loyal Jews into battle against the enemy, and usher in the Final Redemption.

The whole episode will have been a major test of faith, to see which Jews would still believe themselves to be God's people and remain loyal to Him despite the mounting evidence that He was no longer loyal to them. It will turn out, the Midrash says, that the number of such loyalists will be rather small.

Is this Midrash to be taken literally? Will a showdown actually occur between the Jews and the Arabs on the Temple Mount? Will fire literally descend from heaven like in the days of the Mishkan[2] and consume the Arab sacrifice instead of the Jewish one?

Or is the Midrash meant only as a parable, describing what the situation will be like for the Jewish people at the End-of-Days? At the moment it

_____

[2] Portable tabernacle that the Israelites carried with them in the desert after leaving Egypt.

was hard to tell. It certainly looked as if God were favoring the "other side." It was the whole world against the Jewish people, Hezekiah and Sennacherib all over again, except that this time no one expected a miracle like the one God did for the Jewish people of that time. It didn't look good at all for the Jewish state, and the question was how many more Jews would jump ship in fear of being part of the losing side. Even those who hung onto their religion had a difficult time hanging onto their hope.

* * *

It is amazing how sometimes something can be so obvious that no suspects it for what it really is. This can be especially true in the Torah world where there are many righteous people who make sure not to stand out more than others, especially if they are truly unique.

Eli Werster was a rabbi, a third-generation Jerusalem resident who spoke perfect English. He was an older man, somewhere in his sixties, known for his Torah learning and especially for his wonderful character traits. It was hard not to like him. He had a disarming nature, and even secular people who chanced upon him found him pleasantly different.

He didn't have any one particular job, and many wondered how he survived. He would show up at one yeshivah one day, and at another the next. For the most part he kept to himself until the boys of the yeshivah would gradually congregate around him to hear what he had to say. They seemed naturally drawn to Rav Eli, as he was called, and their rabbis didn't mind because of the positive impact he seemed to have.

His wife, righteous in her own right, had passed away several years earlier. The rabbi had children and grandchildren, and they all seemed to be cut from the same holy cloth.

They all appeared to be as humble as their father and grandfather, and they never suspected that the man they called "Abba"[3] or "Zayde"[4] was anything more than their abba or zayde. Special he was, and certainly to them as well, but there was no reason for them to think that he was anything more than he seemed.

The truth is that he thought the same thing about himself. He was grateful for everything he had, and knew how important it was for him to appreciate everything as a gift from God. All his personal success could easily have been personal

---

[3] Father in Hebrew.
[4] Grandfather in Yiddish.

failures if not for the heavenly help he received daily. He was determined to show his gratitude to his Creator by being scrupulous in observance of mitzvot, which he was, and by being a good example to others, which he also was.

In fact he was so unassuming that the significance of his name didn't occur to anyone. Well, hardly anyone. There was a man in his seventies who had known Rav Eli for years, and he felt that Rav Eli was more special than others might have thought. "Righteous people like Elijah," he would say, preferring to call him by his full name, "don't come along very often. We know they are great," he explained to whoever would listen, "but we just don't know how great they really are. They keep that to themselves."

One day he was proven right, because that day Rav Eli underwent a change. Although others had been talking about the imminent arrival of the Messiah for years, Rav Eli deliberately chose not to speak about this matter. He would tell others, "Talking about such things has seriously misled people in the past, and it is best to leave it to the Torah sages to decide when we should speak about him. When the Messiah comes," he explained, "they'll let us know."

No matter how much he was pressed, this was the position he always took when it came to the topic of Mashiach and redemption. Thus it was both surprising and eye-opening when Rav Eli did start to speak about both.

"Had he heard something from higher up?" people asked one another.

"Did he know something they didn't?" they wondered to each other.

"Why is Rav Eli all of a sudden talking about Mashiach?"

In quiet moments, he had wondered the same thing himself. What made him change his opinion on the matter? He didn't realize that it was Hashgochah Pratit, Divine Providence, that was leading him in this new direction. He just happened to see things, or hear things, or think things. The issue seemed to take hold of him by itself, and he couldn't escape it. He found himself compelled to speak to others about it, as if it were his personal responsibility to prepare everyone he could reach to be ready for redemption.

It made some people feel uncomfortable. Concern also developed among the staff of some of the yeshivot he frequented, concern that he might draw boys away from their learning. They worried that the students would get caught up in some messianic fervor and forget about everything else. They had no choice, they felt, but to limit Rav Eli's exposure to the boys, and they told him so.

This hurt him a lot, but then the rumors began. People were speaking about miracles being performed by a particular person, and talk that Mashiach had finally arrived. He felt a need to try to find this person and attempt to determine if the rumors were in fact only that. He wasn't sure why it was so important to him.

He didn't have to search very hard. The man actually sought him out, and found him. It would take only one look for Rav Eli to know that the man he had heard about was the real thing. "How can I help?" Rav Eli asked him.

The man smiled knowingly and said, "You already have. You have already been fulfilling your destiny."

"My destiny?" he asked.

"Your destiny," he said, taking Rav Eli's hand in both of his. As he did, Rav Eli all of a sudden felt completely different...certain...as if knew things... and then more things. Everything just fell into place. It seemed as if something deep within him had risen to the surface and taken over.

"Welcome, my friend," the man said reassuringly. "It is time to be who you are truly meant to be...Elijah!"

"Elijah?" he asked, startled. "The prophet?" he said, incredulously. Then, trying to grasp what it might mean, he started to say, "But I haven't even had a single…"

The man continued to smile.

That is when Rav Eli realized, to his utter amazement, what all those intuitions guiding him had actually been.

At that moment he knew exactly what he had to do next.

A 12-MINUTE war? It takes more time just to talk about it. Fights in the school courtyard take a lot longer. Just picking up the phone to declare war could take almost half that time. Communication is quick today, but it still takes time to use it. Only God can be instantaneous.

But then again, this is God's war. Although he has fought in all of them, from the smallest to the largest, it was mostly from behind the scenes. This one, however, was one He had pledged to personally fight in the open. He made that pledge when Amalek first waged war against the Jewish people. There is an age-old expression: "The redemption of God comes in the blink of an eye." That takes a lot less than 12 minutes.

If the enemy forces had known that months of preparation could be wiped out in minutes, they might not have dared to come. If their families had known that they were headed for a war guaranteed to fail, they might have begged them to stay home. Going AWOL has its consequences, but nothing like those from fighting this kind of war. If anyone had known that thousands of years of human history had been solely for the sake of reaching this very moment, they certainly would have changed sides and joined the Jewish one.

In fact some did. Although some Jews went to the other side, some of the other side crossed over to the Jews. They saw enough miracles to recognize the End-of-Days scenario from their early years of schooling, before political correctness kicked God out of the educational system. When they heard about the coming of the Messiah, and that he was Jewish, it was enough for them.

There are four main groups when it comes to redemption, as we learn from what happened in Egypt. The first group waits eagerly for redemption every day, even when it seems far away. When signs of its arrival begin to appear, its members are ready and willing to go with it. This was the group that joined Moses after just a few miracles, even before the plagues began.

The vast majority of Jews at that point, how-ever, were still not convinced. To get them on side Moses had to perform greater miracles, such as the first few plagues. But they too represented a small group, with the majority still believing that Moses, who grew up in Pharaoh's court, was more a magician than a redeemer. They held out for more.

While they did, they didn't realize that they were also reducing their free will, and therefore the reward for their choice. The greater the mira-cle, the greater the revelation of God, the less diffi-cult the choice is to believe in and follow Him. It can be compared to getting the answers for an exam before writing it. Faith in God requires one to believe in God despite the uncertainty, not after it has been dispelled.

Nevertheless, God wanted as many Jews as possible to leave Egypt. So to encourage more to cross over and join the redemption, Moses did even greater miracles. As a result, more Jews be-came convinced and joined his side of the battle. They were the third group of the four.

As for the last group, they weren't even con-vinced by the eighth plague. Therefore they weren't allowed to stick around for the tenth one, which would be executed by God Himself. With such an intense divine revelation, free will would be temporarily suspended. Consequently the fourth group had to be removed by the ninth plague, the Plague of Darkness, and it was.

The idea itself is frightening. Even more frightening is the fact that this group constituted 80 percent of the Jewish population of that time. Twelve million Jews died in the ninth plague because they refused to believe that the time for redemption had come. As if that weren't bad enough, the Talmud says that a similar scenario will occur at the End-of-Days.

* * *

All visual communications showed the same thing: a middle-aged man with a long beard sitting at a table, looking into the camera. He wore glasses and a black hat. There was nothing distinctive about the way he looked but there was no mistaking that he was Jewish, and Orthodox too.

"Mr. President, you should see this," an aide said.

The president looked up and scrutinized the vision before him. He did not recall seeing that man before, and asked his aide, "Who is this guy? How did he get on the network?"

Another aide in the room answered the question while still listening to his cell. "They've hacked into every visual media around the world!"

The president looked back at the image again and scrutinized it more carefully. Still no recognition. "How is that possible?" he asked.

"We don't know, sir," the aide said, as the secretary of defense burst through the door.

"They've got control of all the networks. All of them!" the defense secretary said.

The phone rang. The president picked it up on the first ring.

"Are you seeing this?" the vice-president asked.

"Do we know who this guy is and what he wants?" the president replied. The answer, however, came from the large screen on the wall of the situation room.

"I understand that this message is being seen all around the world," Elijah said calmly. "I also understand that it will be translated into all languages as I speak. That is good, because the message I have to deliver is for all mankind."

The president sat back in his chair, eyeing the simple person before him, oblivious of how many times the door of the room opened and closed. The entire cabinet had assembled in the same place, and they now listened together to the message.

"What I have to say is simple," Elijah said. "What each of you will do with it is another story. You have only three hours to make your decision."

No one said anything, not in the situation room in the United States nor in any other place around the world. As people watched from their homes, offices, schools, anywhere with a screen, they anxiously waited to hear what the man had to say. Generals on both sides of the war watched from the front lines, while soldiers listened from whatever portable device they could get their hands on. Everyone who was able to listen was listening.

From where he was sitting, he could see no one other than the cameraman and a small staff. He could only imagine how many people were listening to him, but that mattered less to him than saying what had to be said. He had no notes and no one prompting him. He didn't have to look for the words to use, but rather waited for the words to find him.

In Italy the Pope watched with a sense of amusement and trepidation. Thousands of years of squabbling over the identity of God's chosen people, which included many brutal and bloody Crusades, were about to come to an end. Only an hour ago he had thought it was in his favor. Now he was starting to have doubts, a religious leader's worst enemy. For the first time in his entire career he wondered, at least for a moment, if he were actually on the wrong side.

The ayatollahs didn't have the same capacity for even a little self-doubt. They simply couldn't be wrong even when they were. An End-of-Days scenario is what they had been living for. They saw the end of mankind as the threshold to the next era, which they were absolutely certain would belong only to them. If they could hurry it along, so much the better.

The current ayatollah was no different from his irrational predecessors. In fact, hearing that the "Zionist dogs" had taken over all the networks only made him angrier. Seeing one on the screen talking to the entire world pushed him close to the point of no return. He had shown restraint until now, in deference to the American President, but he had his limit. He was about to go past it.

"Give the command to ready the missiles for launch," he said to his aide, who smiled when he heard the words. It was if he had been waiting every day for just such a command.

"Shouldn't we first consult with the president?" another in the room asked, slowing down the messenger.

This angered the ayatollah, although he tried not to show it. "Our president has made promises that we cannot keep," he countered. "I fear that he lacks the religious will to do what our faith tells us we must do." He paused for a moment and, looking in the direction of the voice, asked in an intimidating tone, "Do you as well?"

It worked. The man backed down and the messenger once more was happily on his way to Armageddon.

"Turn it off," the ayatollah motioned to another aide by the large screen on the wall. "There is nothing the Zionist dogs have to say that we need to hear..." and then he added rather confidently, "except that they are no longer with us in this world." He chuckled with the others around him.

* * *

"I have come in the name of God, the God of the Jewish people," Elijah began. "I know this sounds old-fashioned to many of you. I know that many of you simply do not believe that He exists, or that His Torah was given to man at Mt. Sinai thousands of years ago. It has been a long history. Many things have happened to make people doubt His existence, or His supervision. I am here, however, to assure you that He is not only real, but that He is about to reveal Himself to mankind on a level that has not been witnessed for thousands of years."

"Is this guy for real?" the vice-president asked out loud. The same question was being asked in countless places around the globe, and in many different languages. It was the way people answered the question that made them different from each other.

Elijah paused, and then said, "Yes, this is for real."

The vice-president was taken aback, as were the other people who had asked the same question. They all wondered if it were mere coincidence, or if the guy on the screen somehow had a way of knowing what they were thinking.

"You may have heard that Mashiach has come, or, as many call him, 'the Messiah.' These are not rumors. It is the truth, and he has come to redeem the Jewish people and those worthy of being redeemed."

He paused and looked more intensely into the lens, as if he could see the people on the other side.

"In case you do not know what this means, I will explain it to you."

He paused again, and then continued.

"It means that the war you are planning against the Jewish nation will not end in your favor. It means that anyone who chooses from this time onward to continue to try to harm the Jewish nation will be considered as one who has gone to war against God Himself. You will suffer the consequences, and swiftly, as has happened in the past. Do you remember Sancheriv?"

On one hand, the president thought to himself, this guy seems like a religious wacko. On the other hand there is something very real about him and his message. Should he heed the words of the man and stop the war at this point? Or ignore them, give the command to continue the attack, and wait to see what would happen?

"Sir," one of his aides excitedly, "intel shows movement in Iran. Nuclear."

"They're going after Israel," the defense secretary blurted out.

"Get the President of Iran on the line immediately!" the American President barked.

"Sir!" another voice soon yelled back, "all communication in and out of Iran is offline."

"What?"

The American President sat back in his chair. He hadn't seen this coming. He had thought he could keep Iran in line. Now it was about to jeopardize everything and with a lot international troops in the line of fire. He had to think quickly.

"Can we bomb the silo before it launches?"

the president asked.

It was too late.

"Iranian missile launched!" someone yelled out, at the exact moment someone was shouting the same words in Israel.

DOES ISRAEL HAVE the bomb? That was the question many in the military establishment were asking in the 1950s. The question was revised in the 1960s to "How many nuclear bombs does the Jewish state actually have?" In the 1970s the question was "Can Israel deliver its bombs if it wants to?"

It's not a simple matter to launch a nuclear missile. If one is launched from a silo, it usually has to travel a great distance to reach its target. This means that the missile has to travel up as it travels out, just as a ball does when thrown a long distance, in order to overcome the effect of gravity. It also means that the missile is vulnerable to being intercepted before it has time to reach its intended target.

If the bomb is being delivered by aircraft, the plane has to be able to reach its destination without being shot down first. Even if a plane carrying such a dangerous payload were to make it into the air, detection and response time are so quick these days that the bombs would more than likely not be able to get to their targets without major air protection, something the Israelis just didn't have.

That is why there had been a theory for many years that the Israelis, aware of these drawbacks, had smuggled parts of nuclear bombs into major cities around the world for local assembly. Hiding them in important world centers took care of the delivery problem, giving Israel the advantages of a superpower without its actually being one. Some say that the Yom Kippur War ended so suddenly because the Israelis threatened to blow up cities like Washington and Moscow.

It's a good theory that might even be fact. But what no one seemed to consider was what the Israelis were doing back home to protect their borders in the event of a cataclysmic assault, like the one about to take place. Never a country to rely on a single idea for survival, the Israelis always had at least one backup plan. It was one that apparently no one had considered.

Ironically, the idea for the plan came from three unlikely contributors: North Korea, Hezbollah, and Hamas. Hezbollah and Hamas turned the attention of the Israelis' to underground tunnels, and knowledge of North Korea's underground nuclear testing consolidated the scheme. The result was a network of perfectly engineered and precisely placed nuclear charges along the Jordan Valley fault line. After Ariel Sharon gave the Gaza Strip to the Palestinians, the same thing was done along that border as well.

In fact one of the main concerns created by the Hamas tunnel network was not the infiltration of terrorists into the Jewish state. That was definitely a major concern, but one that the Israeli military felt it had solved more or less years before. The greater concern was that Hamas might dig too deep and break into a deeper Israel tunnel, a nuclear chamber, which would reveal everything.

To avoid detection, the Israelis decided to work on expanding a legitimate network of tunnels around the country, either to extend railway lines or to add new roads. Although they purchased far more drilling equipment than was needed, the new construction was so obvious that apparently no one really noticed the extra equipment that was purchased.

The thinking was as follows. If push came to shove and the IDF and IAF couldn't protect their borders, the Israelis would destroy them, the borders, that is. Carefully placed nuclear devices would be detonated underground along the Jordan Valley fault line, triggering an earthquake along the entire Israeli border. There would likely be some collateral damage but if the engineers were correct, it would be minimal on the Israeli side.

IF they were correct. The truth is that no one had any idea if the system would work or whether it might in fact destroy the entire area. It's not as if earthquakes can be controlled, even when man-made. There are many factors that cannot be calculated in advance, and this scheme was definitely a last resort. However, the time for the last resort was fast approaching.

* * *

The American general was baffled. So was everyone around him. The Israelis were retreating and they couldn't imagine why. The nuclear bomb launched by Iran had blown up just before it began its descent for Israel. While everyone was panicking, the bomb inexplicably blew up. That was enough of a mystery for one day, the general thought to himself. Now the Israel Defense Forces were making a hasty retreat. Why?

In Iran, it is always about the evil Zionists. The Iranians were short one nuclear device, internationally humiliated, in deep trouble with their American ally, and no one in Iran knew how it happened. But however it happened, it had to be the fault of the Israelis, the Iranians said. Who else could have pulled off something so despicable, yet technologically advanced...and gotten away with it?

The only thing wrong with the reasoning was that the Israelis themselves were puzzled by what happened. They had tracked the missile from the moment it was fired, and scrambled to find a way to detonate it in the upper atmosphere. If it exploded within 40 miles of the ground, it would cause an EMP, an electromagnetic pulse that could leave Israel without any electricity for miles around, and militarily more vulnerable than it already was.

Mysteriously, the missile seemed to take care of itself. Some even thanked God.

"Are they surrendering?" a British general asked his American counterpart.

"I don't see any white flags," a French general answered instead. "If they are surrendering, shouldn't they simply come out with their hands up?"

"Correct," the American general concurred. "What does packing up and leaving the front do for them? It's as they're afraid of something...but what? They certainly didn't seem to be afraid of us!"

They were asking similar questions back in Washington. There was nothing to indicate that the Israelis were backing down. So why did it look as if they were? The president did not know why, but the whole thing made him feel very uneasy.

In Israel they were asking different questions.

"How much longer before everyone is out of range?" the prime minister asked.

"An hour," the Israeli general answered.

"And the area of impact?"

"It is really impossible to know," the general said. "There was no way to test this plan at all in advance. It's just best guess..."

The prime minister thought for a moment. He was used to precision when it came to Israeli military plans and missions. This one was at best sketchy and therefore very unnerving.

"Worst-case scenario?" the PM finally asked.

"Worst-case scenario?" the general repeated, as if buying time to come up with a suitable answer. He couldn't, so he just told the truth: "A chain reaction that could reach as far as Iran."

"Iran? Wouldn't that be something!" another high-ranking official blurted out.

"It would be," the general said, "if not for all the countries in between."

"So," a cabinet minister asked somewhat sarcastically, "by trying to avoid Armageddon, we may actually cause it?"

"Well," the PM responded just as sarcastically, "only to half the world. The other half will probably stay intact."

"Not according to this guy," said a voice on the other side of the room. Elijah was back on television.

Instantly all eyes turned to the screen and the familiar but unwanted face.

"Not this guy again," a minister said.

* * *

Six thousand miles away they were saying the same thing.

"Still no idea how he's doing it?" the president asked the people around him. "We are supposed to have the most sophisticated security community in the world, and it can't figure out how some religious nut has hijacked international airwaves?"

"Mr. President," someone answered, "we have

tried every means to block the signal but nothing works."

"What does that mean, 'nothing works?'" the president asked, sounding increasingly more impatient. "We don't have the technology to stop a simple person who probably knows as much about technology as my grandmother? And she's already dead!"

For the people to whom the question was posed, there was frustration and humiliation. Everyone else just snickered to themselves.

"Mr. President," another voice volunteered, "we do have the technology. It just isn't working!"

"Let me explain," the secretary of homeland security cut in. "The technology is working, just not the way it is supposed to. It's...it's a..."

All the people in the room, about 21 altogether, were waiting for the secretary to finish his sentence. The secretary himself was looking for the right word, and to his amazement the word "miracle" came to mind. At the same time he knew that it was not the word the president wanted to hear, so he just said, "It's not normal."

"I have come to tell you that your time is now up," Elijah said in a serious voice. "You were given the opportunity to make a decision about where you stand with respect to God and His people. Now you will see if the decision you made is the correct one. It was God's anointed who destroyed the missile just sent against the Jewish people, and it is God's anointed who is now preparing the world for the Messianic Era."

"Is this guy for real?" the vice-president asked. "Is he actually taking credit for the malfunction of the Iranian missile?"

Elijah paused. Then looking into the lens one more time, he added, "The next time anyone will hear from me the world will be a different place. A very different place."

Instantly the screen went blank. This time it was followed by silence just about everywhere, but most noticeably in the Oval Office. No one knew what to say, or whether the guy were a nut case or the real deal. Something seemed to be saying, "Real deal!"

* * *

"Well, that was spooky," an Israeli politician said to his aide. "I wonder what he plans to do...this Elijah character," he said facetiously, "hit us all over the head with his fringes?"

He had barely finished the last word when the entire office building experienced a huge shift, and all of a sudden there was a terrible sound of metal twisting. "This is definitely spoo..." This time he didn't even finish the his last word because the floor collapsed beneath him and he disappeared. He wasn't the only one.

* * *

"Sir!" an officer yelled out, "we are tracking major underground explosions!"

"What?" the American general at the front snapped back. "Where?"

Pointing at a screen of pulsating red circles, the officer said, "Here, here, and here..." He barely finished his sentence when another pulsating red circle showed up on the screen and he added, "and here!"

The general quickly studied the screen and instantly noticed the pattern. The bombs were going off all along the Israeli border. At the same time he realized why the Israelis had retreated without surrendering. "An earthquake..." he said to himself as if having a revelation. Then he turned to the rest of the brass at the table, "My God," he said in horror, "they're setting off an earthquake!"

He looked down towards his feet as he felt the earth beginning to shake below him. Immediately everyone ran for cover.

* * *

"WHAT do you mean, no one detonated the bombs?" the Israeli general yelled into his phone. "SOMEONE had to press that button!"

Suddenly and involuntarily the general turned towards the screen he had been watching just moments ago. Incredulous, he wondered if that guy on the screen also had the ability to set off the underground devices. But how could he have known about them? How could he have set them off?

He didn't have time to consider the answer because an aide ran into the room yelling, "SHOCK WAVES all over the country!" Catching his breath, he shouted, "There are buildings collapsing everywhere!"

He was not completely accurate, however. There were many places that were not affected by the earthquake. It was having a very wide effect, but also an abnormally weird one, as if it were choosing where to go...as if it were being selective.

SOCIAL MEDIA IS great when it works to your advantage. Many people over the years, however, have come to hate it. Once upon a time when you made a mistake out of the public eye, that's where it stayed. With social media the public eye now invades privacy.

A famous rabbi once said that the only reason for the establishment of the UN was in order for it to vote the State of Israel into existence. As the Vilna Gaon explained, if the Jewish people do not merit to be redeemed in a straightforward manner, then redemption has to come with the permission of the nations of the world. Bringing them altogether for a single vote is much simpler than having to deal with each one separately.

Likewise, social media may also have come into existence for this very moment. Everything else it has done until now may have been just to perfect itself for this moment, THE moment, the one for which history had been waiting thousands of years. The end was not just near. The end had arrived.

* * *

The American President was so shocked by what he was watching and hearing that he didn't bother to consider how it was even possible to provide such a view. There were no military satellites in the area that could take those shots, and the commercial ones, by law, did not have high enough resolution. How it was filmed really didn't make a difference to anyone, however, because the sight was totally bizarre. Even disaster movies weren't filmed this well.

In the Oval Office there was just stunned silence. So also in just about every office and home around the world where people were watching the same scene. They had no choice. Exactly the same event was on Facebook, Twitter, Instagram, and other social media. It was even on computer screens that weren't connected to the internet. How was that possible?

"What the…?" was a common question around the world.

"What kind of hack is this?" was one of the friendlier responses. The people in the bars whose favorite sports games were interrupted had less polite things to say...until they realized, that is, what they were looking at. Then no one said anything.

* * *

The cavity in the earth just kept moving north and south along the eastern Israeli border. The same thing was happening east and west on the Egyptian and Lebanese borders. It also kept getting wider as it moved along. The truly horrifying part was seeing tanks and trucks just fall into the abyss, hundreds of them, thousands of them, all over the place. Entire bases were swallowed and people had nowhere to run. Watching it was torture but not looking was even worse.

Every national leader whose country had sent troops to the front was forced to witness the ground swallowing up those very troops. The sense of hopelessness was overwhelming. The British Prime Minister had tears in his eyes. The French President muttered to himself over and over again. They all wanted to reach out through their screens and rescue people, or at least call for a retreat. They knew the situation was hopeless.

The only exception was the Canadian Prime Minister. He had refused to participate in a war against Israel and had fought hard in Parliament to avoid it. He had to survive two no-confidence votes, and even that resulted in a compromise with the opposition leader. Canadian troops would remain on standby in case they had to join the conflict in a hurry.

Now the leader of the opposition was calling the prime minister, his hand shaking. He was thinking how he would have been feeling right now had he been forced to watch Canadian troops meet the same fate, troops that he had fought so hard to send in order to save Canada's face. Somberly, he thanked the prime minister for standing by his convictions.

* * *

In Israel the mood was even more confused. The "believers" had been waiting for such a miracle. They had expected such a miracle. But they still had a hard time believing that they were actually witnessing the miracle.

The disbelievers were in total shock. Some who had yarmulkes put them on. Others went in search of them. Many cried out in fear of what it meant for them personally. God may be alive and well after all, they realized, and Torah is indeed an obligation. Now what?

The Israeli government was on high alert. There was a fear of reprisals, but they were looking less likely each moment, at least locally. There were the IBMs, but would they use them so close to their own troops? What was the White House doing? What was the Kremlin planning? What was anyone's next move?

* * *

"What are the losses?" the president asked his general. He was somber, very somber.

"Total, Mr. President."

"Everyone and everything?" he asked completely incredulous.

The general shook his head in disbelief. He had never before felt like crying. He had gone through many wars and seen many losses, but he had always fought the urge to show any emotion. That is partly why he was chosen for the top military job. He was known as someone who could get the job done while remaining even-keeled. But he was not at all even-keeled now.

"Just about everyone..." the general said with

a voice of resignation, "and just about every-thing..."

"The fleets?" the president asked hesitantly.

The general answered, "The Gulf Fleet took heavy losses...some kind of tsunami from the earthquake. The Mediterranean Fleet is intact..." he paused before saying the next thing. The president could see he had more to say.

"What is it?"

"Mr. President, the crew is spooked."

"Spooked?" the vice-president cut in.

"Well, everyone can see what has been happening. There are religious men on these ships. They really think that all this is the hand of God. They're afraid to fight."

"Afraid to fight?" the president asked sharply as he got up from his chair and went to a large picture window. It overlooked a perfectly manicured White House garden that bespoke of more normal times. Now it seemed completely out of synch with the current reality.

"And you, General?" he asked looking out the window. "What do you think? Is it the hand of God?"

The general looked at the others in the room whose own expressions suggested the same confusion.

"Mr. President," he finally said, "you know that

I am not a religious man, not by any stretch of the imagination. Do I believe in God? I really don't know. When you've fought as many battles as I have, you're bound to see what some call miracles. But," he qualified, "all the death and dying quickly wipes that away. However," he qualified again, "today?" he said shaking his head in disbelief, "I have never ever seen anything like it! Frankly sir, I don't know what to think."

There was quiet in the room.

"Could the Israelis have done this?" the president asked, still looking out the window.

The general thought for a moment, and then offered, "In my opinion, I don't think so. The earthquake is following a very specific path...even where the fault line does not extend. How could they possibly do that?

The president thought for a moment. He turned around and asked everyone in the room, "Could this have been...a so-called 'act of God,' and by 'act of God,' I mean the natural type?"

No one knew what to answer. Finally a voice that seemed to come from the back of the room called out, "No, Mr. President."

No one recognized the voice, and they all turned to see who spoke. At first they couldn't find the source of the voice, until they realized that it came from the video screen on the wall.

Impossible!

After recovering from their shock, the first thing that occurred to everyone was that it was pure coincidence that the voice spoke at just the right moment. The person on the screen wasn't actually addressing the president as if they were in a video conference. The rabbi, or whoever he was, was obviously broadcasting to a wide audience and making a general statement.

Or so they thought.

"Yes, Mr. President," the voice said. "I can see you."

People looked at each other.

"He's just making that up," the secretary of state said mockingly.

"No I'm not, Mr. Secretary," the person on the screen replied, and the secretary's mouth dropped open.

"If you like, I can tell you where you are sitting, Mr. President, what you are wearing, how many people are in the room with you…"

"How...how can you do that?" the president asked, feeling exposed.

The man on the screen just smiled. "A miracle," he said.

Everyone in the room was silent.

Everyone around the world was silent.

"What do you want?" the American President

asked.

"First allow me to introduce myself, and to introduce you…"

All eyes shifted to the president whose own eyes were transfixed on the screen. What did he mean, "and introduce you?" To whom?

"I have been chosen," the man on the screen explained, "by the God of Israel, to represent His people at this time in history. I am not doing any of this on my own. I have no personal power. Everything I have done is from God Himself, and the miracles that I have performed are His."

The president looked at his top advisors. Was this guy crazy? Talented, but crazy? Perhaps he's a disgruntled communications techie who is taking personal revenge on the world.

The man on the screen smiled, as if amused by the thought. But he said, "It would be unwise to think like that, and assume that I am simply mentally unfit. Do not ignore what I am saying."

Everyone in the Oval Office looked at each other again in wonder. The president asked himself, "How could this guy know such things? Is there someone in the room relaying information to him?"

"You can check, if you'd like," the man on the screen said. "But you will find that everyone in the room is loyal to you, not to me, which is a problem for them."

The president looked embarrassed. He hadn't tweeted, yet his opinion was instantly known around the world. He had doubted his staff.

"This is the important point," the man continued. "Have you heard the name 'Gog' before?"

"Gog?" the secretary of state asked out loud. Looking at the president, he said, "That's the biblical character who causes Armageddon!"

"Correct, Mr. Secretary," the man in the screen said, looking in the direction of the secretary as if he could see him. He could, in his mind's eye.

"Mr. President," the man on the screen said gravely, "Do you wish to be Gog?"

"What do you mean?" the president asked defensively. He was the leader of the world's greatest superpower, but he was being led around by some unknown Orthodox rabbi over a video screen.

"The war you have been leading is not just any war. You have waged it to force the Jewish people to surrender their holy land to a gentile nation. God has waged it as the last battle of history, what Judaism refers to as the 'War of Gog and Magog.' It is meant to be the last war the world will ever see."

Mashiach paused for a moment to allow the

world to catch up to him. Then he continued, "You may find this very hard to believe, but what is known in English as the 'Messianic Period' has in fact begun. Therefore, if you cease your hostility and instead instruct your people to repent to the God of Israel, everything can proceed smoothly."

"You're talking about countless other religions and billions of Muslims!" the president responded. "How am I supposed to change their minds—if I am to change their minds?"

The enormity of the problem only made it seem more ridiculous, so he continued, "And if I don't?"

"Then I advise you to pick up a book of the Prophets," Mashiach said, "what you call 'Isaiah.' You should carefully read about Gog...and his future."

The president looked at his advisors. For the first time ever they felt out of their league. Everything was surreal. Incredibly surreal. There was something authentically End-of-Daysish about this guy. They didn't know what to say or do next.

The choice is yours, Mr. President," Mashiach warned. "It will be your last one."

Then the screen went blank, as screens did all over the world at the same moment.

Within minutes there were disagreements throughout the world. Some people demanded that the UN forces withdraw immediately and leave Israel alone. God or no God, Messiah or no Messiah, the situation was way out of hand. Backing down seemed the safest bet.

Others warned about the End-of-Days and divine judgment. There were normal people and there were crazy ones, but they all said basically the same thing. The Bible had predicted such times. Now they were living them.

And then there were those who remained unfazed. They demanded that the president finish the job he started. They saw the whole message as religious rhetoric and coercion. They didn't care about how weird the situation was. Their hatred of religion and Jews went beyond logic and demanded revenge.

* * *

The president asked everyone to leave the room. He also asked for a copy of Isaiah. When he was alone, he made a call to his religious mentor of years back. He needed some religious insight and advice for a change, and fast.

* * *

"He will not back down," Elijah said to Mashiach.

"No, he will not," he answered. "The end is truly here, and the beginning has just begun."

Kvar

A PERSON CAN live 80 or 90 years, and yet his entire life can hinge on a single decision. He or she can make it earlier or later but, once made, such a decision puts the person on course for either personal success or failure. In some circumstances, it can even cause global damage.

For the current President of the United States, that decision came when he was only 14 years old. It was then that he developed an ambition to one day become the leader of the United States of America, by hook or by crook. Although no one around him at the time took his dream seriously, from that point on he never wavered.

He would not be just any president. He would be the one to finally bring about world peace. He would be the first president bold enough to make the necessary changes to society at large to remove the "demons" that foster hate and cause war. The adults were amused by his naive idealism, but nothing more.

Only one person actually took note of the up-and-coming politician and decided to help him on his way. It wasn't that his benefactor saw eye to eye with his future candidate for the White House. It was rather that he saw someone he could work with to accomplish his own secret agenda.

It was a match made in heaven or, more likely, the other place. Both men were narcissistic and arrogant. The only major difference between the two was that one contentedly worked from behind the scenes, while the other was the front man. Together they would one day be known as "Gog and Magog."

Or at least the American portion of it. On the other side of the world there was someone who combined both elements in one person while leading the other major superpower. The Prime Minister of Russia was wealthy, ambitious, and every bit as narcissistic and arrogant as his American counterparts, if not more so. He was certainly more ruthless. From a young age he too had planned to use every political resource at his disposal, but his goal was to restore the grandeur that was once Mother Russia. And then some.

When the President of the United States first took office, the Russian Prime Minister saw only opportunity. Just as the Japanese took advantage of Roosevelt's pacifism to seriously disable the Americans in World War II, the Russian PM saw the current American President's misguided pacifism as Russia's gateway to world domination.

There is a tradition that the biblical Magog can be traced back in time, and migrated to somewhere near what today is Moscow. The Russian leader, unaware of and certainly not caring about such a tradition, was intent only on fulfilling his country's destiny, and his at the same time. Egotism is blinding on all sides of the world.

However, the moment the American President refused to back down and instead decided to travel to the scene of the conflict, history shifted. His heart prompted the decision, his brain made it, and his mouth verbalized it to the others around him. But it was a decision that sent a strong signal to heaven that Gog was alive and well and ready to make history. A special soul descended by "return mail" to give the American leader the spiritual wherewithal to fulfill his destiny on a biblical level.

As the president boarded Air Force One, he felt a great sense of mission. He wasn't sure why, but despite the fact that so many troops and weapons had been lost, it didn't bother him as much as it should have. He was focused on getting the job done, and he just assumed that after he was successful, all would be forgiven and he would be the hero.

His wife had tried to convince him not to go, and when he refused to listen, she insisted on accompanying him. He refused this as well, citing the safety of their children as her chief priority at the time. If all went well, and he sensed that it would, he would be back before the end of the week and would receive a Nobel Peace Prize for his commitment and determination to stabilize the world.

Then she said something very strange, and she wasn't even sure why those words left her mouth. "Maybe you really can't fight the Jews."

The president looked at his wife, who appeared just as confused as he felt. "Where did that come from?" his gaze said, while hers said, "I don't know."

The truth is that her words were similar to those said by Haman's wife when her husband planned to do the same thing to the Jews of his time. Zeresh had warned him that if Mordechai were descended from Yehudah, his plan would backfire on him, and it did. It was an unusual statement to come from the wife of one of the Jewish people's greatest enemies ever, but it was 100 percent correct.

What his wife said didn't make any difference whatsoever to the president, who was completely possessed by his mission. He felt heroic and drawn into the conflict and, not believing in the Jewish God or the uniqueness of His people, he just couldn't see it for what it was. He couldn't see what he was becoming, what he had already become, although even his wife suspected something.

So the president boarded Air Force One as the flight crew went over the final checklist and flight plan. F-16s were scheduled to accompany the president's plane the entire way. In order to avoid Israeli airspace, it was decided to fly over Egypt and then over Jordan. There were some severe weather warnings, but they were far enough away from the flight path to be ignored.

Once POTUS and his entourage were settled in, Air Force One began to move toward the runway. Security was tight as always, and even the media wouldn't be told about the president's trip until after he landed. Everything was proceeding as planned.

As the president and his team discussed their options of how to finally subdue the Israeli military and remove its government, they really had no idea what to expect once they arrived. Strange things had been happening, most of them inexplicable. That was one of the first things the generals wanted to investigate and deal with after they took control of the Jewish state.

It costs the Air Force about $210,880 an hour to operate the president's plane. It had a range of 6,800 nautical miles and a cruising speed of 575 mph at a height of 35,000 feet. At just over 6,000 miles flying distance, amounting to about eleven hours of flight time, the US taxpayers would be forking up just under $2.5 million for the flight.

That figure, however, was only four percent of the actual cost of the trip, a fact which might not have been relevant had everything gone according to plan.

Secrecy has both advantages and disadvantages, like most everything else. Some of the best and worst scenarios in history have occurred because people were left out of the loop. The story of the president is an example of both.

* * *

The Khomeinis have never been known for their cool-headedness. Nor are they famous for a spiritually balanced point of view. They live each day with the fanatical belief that they are the "chosen ones," that God is on their side, and that their version of the Messianic Era is just around an explosive and fiery corner. If they were to have an accurate bumper sticker printed, it would say, "Extremism is us."

One thing you do not do is to best Iran, and how much more so if you are the Jewish state. That's similar to putting pig on the body of a dead Arab terrorist. According to tradition, this would deny the martyr (a.k.a. dangerous religious fanatic) his 72 virgins in the afterlife.

Defeat is not something the Iranians learn from, at least not in any peaceful way. Their first missile blowing up only meant that a second one had to be sent. Sure enough, against all logic and without international permission, they launched a second nuclear missile at the Jewish state, having no idea of the impact it would have on the world.

* * *

The moment the missile was launched, a siren went off in the cockpit of the president's plane. The onboard command center was one of the most sophisticated in the world, despite its minuscule size. Immediately it picked up the Iranian missile, and Langley began issuing instructions.

The president and his staff were notified at once, while evasive action was implemented. Turning around was out of the question. Leaving the area of impact immediately was essential, and that itself created all kinds of logistical and security issues.

The world's militaries weren't the only ones tracking the missile. Within seconds of its launch, every major government had its eyes on the Iranian missile and began preparing for the fallout. The Israelis, however, had to first prepare for the impact. Fallout for them was a secondary issue that would be relevant only if they survived the blast.

Sirens. Panic. Tremendous movement. Israeli life became a blur—again.

Except for two men who were standing at the Kotel. Their lack of movement was completely out of step with the world around them. They were calm, focused. If anyone had noticed them, he or she would have thought that they were completely out of touch with reality, without even considering the possibility that they were completely in control of it.

As the one closed his eyes, he put his left hand on the right arm of the other. Instantly the second man saw what the first saw, not with his physical eyes, however, but with his mind's eye. Together they saw the missile, and the president's plane changing course. The entire scenario unfolded and "flowed" through them like blood in their veins. It was overwhelming and, if not for the hand of the other on his arm, it might have been too overwhelming for Elijah. Instead he felt the calm of the other.

As they stood there, the first one slowly and deliberately raised his hand in the direction of the incoming missile. The second knew this without actually seeing it. As the arm ascended, Elijah could feel a spiritual energy surge through his body in a way never before felt. He could feel the energy stream out and he knew exactly where it went.

Within moments there was a massive explosion in the upper atmosphere. Once again, to the fury of the Iranians, their missile blew up, or was blown up, far away from Israel. Even the Arab nations below were spared damage, or so they thought.

An electromagnetic pulse (EMP) is a short burst of electromagnetic energy. Such a pulse may occur in the form of a radiated electric or magnetic field or a conducted electric current, depending on the source, and it may be natural or man-made...EMP interference is generally disruptive or damaging to electronic equipment, and at higher energy levels a powerful EMP event, such as a lightning strike, can damage physical objects such as buildings and aircraft structures...The damaging effects of high-energy EMP have been used to create EMP weapons. These are typically divided into nuclear and non-nuclear devices. (Wikipedia)

Thanks to technology, today there are many ways to cause massive destruction. Not too long ago it took a major war with a lot of people to wreak havoc to such an extent. Then came the nuclear bomb, which meant that a single plane or ICBM could deliver destruction on a huge scale with minimum human involvement. Major wars could now be fought, and won or lost, at the touch of buttons.

Nevertheless such wars were still outside the means of most countries, resulting in a Cold War that really included only the two largest superpowers at the time. That is the way it basically remained for decades, until terrorism taught the world that even ragtag country-less military groups could bring entire countries to their political knees, or at least cause significant damage.

An EMP attack takes this danger to a whole new and frightening level. Today a rogue nation could launch a nuclear missile from a fishing trawler off the coast of a major country and explode it in the upper atmosphere before planes or missiles could be sent to stop it. This would result in an electromagnetic pulse that could, and more than likely would, knock out much of a country's electrical grid.

Since our lives are heavily automated today, when the electrical systems on which we have come to depend die, people die as well. Lots of people. Most of the people. Perhaps even faster than they might have died during a conventional war. In moments, entire societies could be thrown back to the Dark Ages with little knowledge of how to survive in such times. A few terrorists could, God forbid, destroy an entire nation with an EMP attack.

One place you certainly do not want to be during a local EMP attack, even if it occurs accidentally, is in the air, no matter how big, fast, or expensive the plane is. But that was exactly where the President of the United States of America found himself during the EMP that resulted from the explosion of the Iranian missile. All of a sudden Air Force One was dead, and soon many of its passengers as well.

There were be survivors. The President of the United States was not one of them.

* * *

The two men standing at Western Wall, eyes still closed, knew all this already. It would be a short while before the news reached the rest of the world, especially their fellow Jews, who were panicking around them.

It was not yet over, but it would be soon.

19

Nimtza

IT DIDN'T MAKE sense. The president's plane had been built to withstand an EMP attack, at least from a certain distance. According to the last reported location of Air Force One, the plane should have been out of range, protected. Yet by all accounts, the instant and complete loss of control, including that of the accompanying fighter jets, pointed to the result of an EMP attack.

The head of the snake was now dead. It was time to deal with its body.

* * *

"Are these confirmed reports?" the Israeli PM asked his people.

"From the State Department itself. All the news stations are reporting it."

The prime minister thought. On one hand, the news was too good to be true. On the other hand, if it were true...

"What do they gain by lying?" one of the generals in the room asked.

"A safety precaution?" a military person of lesser rank guessed.

"That's what I want to know," the PM said. "Maybe it's to make us overconfident so we'll let our guard down."

"What guard?" the secretary of defense asked. "We are heavily outnumbered and outgunned. What threat are we to them?"

"Nuclear," the PM answered.

"They know we would never use it," the secretary responded.

"They don't know that we didn't use it already," the general asserted. "They just watched half their army disappear through a large crack in the ground. For all they know, we did that with underground nuclear devices."

"We DID do that with underground nuclear devices!" the secretary shot back.

"They were our bombs, but we didn't set them off," the general said, defensively.

"You know that, and I know that, but..." the

PM began to say before being interrupted. The door burst open and all eyes focused on the man who entered, clearly out of breath.

"It's confirmed…" the man said, trying to catch his breath. "It's confirmed…the president's plane went down. He's dead."

All eyes went back to the prime minister who slowly sat back in his chair. "Well, that changes a lot," he said cautiously. "It changes an awful lot."

* * *

"Son of man!" the voice said.

It was not the first time that he had received prophecy, but it was the first time that the prophecy was being heard by others. Lots of others. In fact, every "other."

One of the most important goals of the Final Redemption is that it can leave no doubt about Who did it. No doubt whatsoever. There has to be 100 percent certainty in the mind of every survivor that God, and no one else and nothing else, saves anything. This is why it was destined to occur with great miracles, miracles so huge that even the most resolute disbelievers would be forced to finally believe. Unfortunately, it would too late for many of them.

* * *

"Are you hearing this?" the news correspondent asked excitedly. He was 6,000 miles away in downtown Cairo.

The man behind the news desk back in New York had a skewed look on his face. The millions of people watching him just assumed that it was because he was trying to figure out what it was he was hearing. They had no idea that it was also because he was freaking out.

"I am getting it," he told the man in the field. "But the weird thing is that it sounds as if I'm hearing it inside my head!"

"Wow!" he responded. "I thought I was the only one!"

The man at the station received a message through his earpiece which he promptly passed on to the millions of viewers around the world who were watching him.

"We're going to take a short break and be right back."

Immediately the screens of the viewers switched to a commercial as the station prepared to return in a few minutes.

"I heard it too," one of the cameramen called.

"Me too!" said another.

"Jim!" the man behind the desk called out,

"Can you extend this break? This is weird and we need some answers before going back online."

"I can give you five minutes," the station director called back, "but not a second more or people will change the channel!"

Bill Williams, the anchor at the desk, turned to the people in the room and asked, "Any ideas?"

They all either shook their head or just had a blank stare. Then a woman's voice called out, "I don't understand how all of us could possibly hear the same thing at once, but I recognize what was said."

All attention turned to the source of the voice, which turned out to be a woman in her 60s. The average age in the room was about 40, so she was definitely the senior in the room.

"What's your name," the anchor asked.

"Margaret," the woman answered, "Margaret Wells."

"What do you do here, I mean at the station, Margaret?"

"I'm in Accounting. I just happened to be in this room when it happened," she explained.

"So," another anchor asked, "What were you saying?"

"Well," Margaret began, insecure from all the attention she was now getting from so many people she admired, "I'm no Bible expert..."

"Okay," the first anchor jumped in, "but what does that have to do with the strange voice in all our heads?"

"Those words..." she said, all of a sudden sounding more serious and firm, "those are the same words that the Lord uses in the Bible to talk to His prophets."

She paused and looked up to see everyone staring at her. It was very disconcerting. But she also noticed that no one was laughing at her. Some even had a look of concern.

"Ah, well," said Bill, the first anchorman, purposely trying to sound calm in order to dilute the intensity of the moment, "that may be true. But," he concluded, "that doesn't quite explain how all of us heard the very same thing at the very same time."

"It could be..." the cameraman began to say, as all eyes shifted from Margaret to Bob, "that if it's really God speaking, then He could do it, right? I mean, He's God, right?"

"Assuming that you believe in God!" Bill said, rather matter-of-factly.

"And you don't?" Margaret asked the anchorman.

Bill thought for a moment. He wanted to answer "no" but sensed that it would cast him in a negative light. "I'm not sure," he said instead.

"Well," an older, stronger voice broke in. All heads turned toward the station owner as he entered the room. "Whether you believe in God or not is less important at this time than the FACT that we're back on the air in 30 seconds."

Everyone scrambled back to their positions. As Bill collected himself, he turned to the station owner and asked him, "Did you hear it too?"

The man stood there, hands in his pockets. He had 20 seconds left to give an answer that could either ease the situation or cause tremendous chaos. He wanted to say "no" but found himself saying "yes" instead.

Bill half smiled as he turned back towards the camera and waited for the red light to tell him he was on the air. With one second left to go, however, he received a different signal. It was the voice again.

* * *

"Son of man!" the voice repeated. "Command the wind. Tell it that it should blow to the east and to the west, to the north, and to the south. Son of man," the voice continued, "command the dirt of the ground to move with the wind and to blow to the four corners of the world, and to become a cloud of darkness and sweep over the face of the earth. It is a cloud of God," the voice explained, "and it will travel the entire world of man. It will determine who is to live and who is to die. The Lord, God of the descendants of Abraham, Isaac, and Jacob has spoken, son of man. The great and awesome day of judgment is here, and it will be decided who shall live and who shall perish, who shall be redeemed and who shall not be redeemed."

Rather than the "son of man" doing exactly what he was told, he was encircled by a wind that began to blow, picking up dirt as it did, and growing in size outward and upward.

* * *

Manny Lefkowitz thought that he was going crazy. The first time he heard the voice he had been distracted, and just wrote it off as a result of too much stress. This time, however, he not only heard the entire message, but his wife heard it too. They looked at each other, and then at their children. They were worried, very worried. Avowed atheists, they had never dreamed that they would have to question their belief, certainly not because of some strange voice in their head.

They didn't say anything. They didn't have to. Their eyes said it all. They felt a mixture of terror, doubt, regret, and a sinking feeling that they had missed the boat, really missed the boat. They didn't know yet how many people around the world were feeling the same way. They were not alone, but definitely felt as if they were.

* * *

The men in the space station could not believe their eyes. They too had heard the voice and were also able to watch the cloud of darkness spread in all directions from the Middle East, including up towards them. By tomorrow at the same time, the world would be entirely different.

20

B'olam

THE MASSIVE BLACK cloud continued to expand as it spread out in all directions. News stations reported on its progress as long as they could but eventually they all fell silent. Cameramen filmed it until it consumed them. All forms of communication just stopped. The entire world was silent.

It was an utterly eerie and ominous scene. People could see the massive cloud rolling in towards them, but they didn't know what to expect. Some chose to watch it from windows, from roofs, from wherever they could get a glimpse of it. They saw it overtake the only world they knew.

Others chose to hide. They went as far as they could possibly get from open spaces, but nothing helped. The cloud entered tunnels, elevator shafts, underground parking lots. Everywhere. Wherever people went, the cloud went too. And wherever the cloud went, there was usually panic and screaming. In some cases there was just total silence.

Even for believers it was a moment of truth. You can fool yourself some of the time, other people most of the time, but God, none of the time. Who actually knew what God really thought of them? Who knew with any certainty who would survive the darkness? These were questions that could only be answered in retrospect, after the cloud had passed, and only by the people who were left alive.

There had been six astronauts on the International Space Station before the cloud reached it. When the cloud left, only two remained, the two who "happened" to have brought Bibles with them. Not even the bodies of the other four remained; they had disappeared like smoke.

The same thing happened all over the earth below. After the cloud passed, the number of people left was significantly smaller than it had been before the cloud came. Those who were gone left no trace. It was as if they had never existed in the first place.

There were plenty of surprises though. Some

people who thought they would not survive did, while some who were certain they would, didn't. Only God knows the totality of a person, including previous reincarnations and all the trials and tribulations of each lifetime. Only His expectations are accurate, and His evaluations are just. Sometimes the people we reject are the very ones whom God praises, and vice-versa.

Not only had the population of the world dwindled enormously, but buildings were missing as well. It wasn't hard to figure out the pattern: If a structure were used for evil, then it disappeared. If it had been used for even a hint of good, it remained standing.

Military installations were the exception. After the cloud passed, every single one ceased to exist altogether. Not even the foundations were spared. War was over forever, and with it went all the physical reminders of the ones that had been fought previously. It was a completely new world, an entirely new era. It was unfathomable.

In some cases entire families remained intact. In other cases they did not. Sometimes only one spouse remained, or a few brothers and sisters, aunts, uncles, or other relatives. Money did not buy safety this time, or preferential treatment either. This time it was about one form of currency only: spiritual merit. Yesterday a person could have mocked belief in God. Today it was only that belief that saved a person from annihilation.

When the cloud left the newsroom, the station was short a few anchor people, as well as other staff. The anchorman who wasn't sure if he believed in God? Missing in action, among the billions of others like him around the world.

As the cloud left each place, the people it passed over became different. They began to just know things. They found that they just happened to understand more, more about the world, more about life, and most important of all, more about God. They no longer had any desire for trivial things, only a powerful yearning for God.

Jews remained around the world, but not the majority of them. It became clear who was halachically Jewish and who was not. If people had sincerely wanted to be Jewish before the cloud came but had been misinformed about the true process of conversion, they could still complete the process halachically. If they had converted for the wrong reasons, with little or no intention to live a Torah lifestyle, their opportunity to survive was lost. Many families were split apart.

All the Jews living in the Diaspora finally had an insatiable desire to return to Eretz Yisroel. Even those who previously had no connection to the Land now knew that it was the only place they could fulfill themselves. They began to make plans to return home.

The cloud that passed through the Holy Land was not black. It was white. Everything the white cloud touched was cleansed of all evil and impurity. As it washed over the Old City of Jerusalem, Jews and Gentiles alike panicked and ran in all directions. Some made it to the Kotel, the Western Wall, and held onto it for dear life, praying for survival. If they had no yarmulke, they found one. If they could not find one, they improvised.

After the cloud passed, not everyone remained at the Kotel. Those who did, however, were astounded by the new reality around them. The Temple Mount had been completely cleared, without a sign of the mosques or their worshippers. Just beyond, on the Mount of Olives, all the churches were gone as well. Not a trace of any other religion remained throughout the entire Land of Israel. Finally it was once again a Torah nation.

Even in the Diaspora, anything or anyone with any connection to idol worship on any level was removed from the world. It was definitely not a good time to be a politician, especially a world leader. Abuse of any kind could not exist in the Messianic Era, nor could abusive people.

Humility had been key. As the cloud passed, it

measured the humility of everyone. If people were sufficiently humble, they survived, and were even spiritually enhanced. If not, they simply disappeared.

* * *

Days had passed since the cloud had dissipated. There was no doubting what had happened or Who had done it. The world had not only become an ideal place, it had become a perfect place. As perfect as a physical world could become.

It was a good time to be a Jew. Antisemitism, all of it, had died with the antisemites. The billions of people who remained could not do enough to help the Jews around them to act as the "Kingdom of Priests" they had been destined to become, on behalf of ALL mankind.

Now the Gentiles wanted the Jews to leave their lands, but not because they didn't want them to stay. They definitely did want them to stay. But each knew in his or her heart that the Jewish people had a special God-given mission, and that they belonged in Israel. It was their role, they knew, to help the Diaspora Jews get there. They understood that history could not complete its destiny, nor they theirs, until all the remaining Diaspora Jews returned home.

And return they did.

By plane.

By train.

By boat.

Quite quickly millions of Jews began to converge on the land of their ancestors. They were greeted with open arms, and everything that could be done to soften the transition was put in place. Families were reunited, friends embraced, and tears flowed. Had it been a movie, it would have been beyond belief.

Mr. Kuperman was 85 years old and had to be taken from the plane by wheelchair. As the attendant pushed him to the waiting area, he seemed relaxed, making small talk, smiling, and waving at little children along the way.

There was no customs clearance since there was no longer any need for it. The attendant just wheeled Mr. Kuperman through the large electric doors into a mob of waiting families and friends.

Halfway across the arrivals area, Mr. Kuperman asked his attendant to stop the wheelchair, although he had no idea why. Then he stood up, raised his eyes to the ceiling, stretched out his arms, and, falling to his knees, yelled at the top of his lungs:

"SHEMA YISROEL, HASHEM ELOKEINU, HASHEM ECHAD—HEAR O ISRAEL, THE LORD OUR GOD, THE LORD IS ONE!"

Heads turned towards the voice. Some weren't sure whether or not it was just an old man losing it, which is exactly what they would have thought only a few months earlier. But now, seeing the old man on his knees, arms still stretched towards heaven, they realized the truth of what he had said. Silence spread throughout the large hall.

Suddenly a much younger voice yelled out the same words from across the room, and then another, and another. So many people were saying "Shema" at the same time that the atmosphere became electric. It expressed what was felt not just there, but around the world as well.

Now it was clear why so much construction had occurred over the previous few years, despite the fact that the Intifada had intimidated many from making aliyah. The once half-empty airport handled the many planes arriving from around the world, the once seemingly frivolous highway expansions now carried the greatly increased traffic, and the new high-speed trains allowed Jews to reach different parts of the country more efficiently.

God had been preparing for the ingathering

of exiles right under our noses, and few even had a clue.

*   *   *

Abraham and his wife of 60 years, Rachel, could not hold back their tears. They had survived Auschwitz and Treblinka, and made it to Israel despite the British blockade. They had started with absolutely nothing and, against the odds, built a family from scratch. In the process they had returned to the religion of their fathers when they became Torah observant.

Some of their children had gone to yeshivah, some to the army, and some to both. Abraham himself had fought in four wars and survived them all. Tragically, two of his sons had not been so fortunate, but had died as heroes, defending their country. The rest had grown up, married, and begun families of their own.

The Lichtensteins had known struggle. They knew suffering. They also knew the meaning of great loss firsthand. What they had not known was that, after all they had gone through and survived, they would witness the Messianic Era.

Abraham had not seen his brother Jonathan, also a survivor, for over 30 years, Rachel, her sister Miriam for 25 years. They had kept in touch as best they could, but not being tech savvy they resorted to occasional telephone calls and snail mail.

Until a few days ago they had not even been sure that their siblings had survived the cloud. Now both Jonathan and Miriam were on their way to them along with their families. Abraham and Rachel didn't know how to handle the joy, especially when they saw the faces of their long-lost siblings.

Abraham couldn't control himself. He ran to Jonathan and hugged him with every bit of energy he had. He kissed him and cried, as did his brother. Then they joined hands and started dancing, singing through their tears, "Am Yisroel Chai![1] Am Yisroel Chai!" They were joined by countless others, some waving fists in the air as if in defiance all of those who ever tried to put an end to the Jewish people.

*   *   *

Unlike many of its staff members, both the White House and the Kremlin survived. Gone, however, were the security fences and any vestige of their former days. Instead the people trans-

---

[1] The people of Israel live.

formed these places and others like them into places of worship of God, the One true God, the God of Israel. Everyone knew that now, and this brought them much closer to the next great event.

In the meantime Jerusalem had swelled beyond its city limits. People found shelter wherever they could and, if necessary, camped out in places like the forest. There was no need to fear anyone or anything any more. The yetzer hara[2] was gone and with it all the vices of man. People learned Torah together, prayed together, and waited together. They would not have to wait much longer.

* * *

"Samuel, do you hear that?"

"Hear what?" Samuel said, rubbing his eyes, looking at the time on his watch, and then at his little brother. It was dark outside, but his watch said that it would soon be light.

"That!" little David said, as the noise became less faint.

Samuel could barely hear it at first, and he listened more intently. There was no mistaking the sound. It was a shofar. No, it was many shofars. He jumped to his feet and quickly washed his hands,

---

[2] Inclination to do evil.

and as he did, a great commotion began in his house.

"Come on! Everyone get up!" their father called to them as he ran past their bedroom door. "It's coming! It's coming!"

Quickly dressing, the boys joined their father for morning prayers. It was a quick walk to the synagogue, especially with a bounce in their step. The place was already packed when they arrived and everyone was excited. The atmosphere was electric.

After the service the men broke into spontaneous dance. In fact, the same thing was happening in countless places around the country. The dancing continued until they heard another shofar blowing, except this time it kept getting stronger and stronger. They not only heard it, they felt it, and it energized their bodies as they took to the streets.

All of a sudden, someone looked up and called out, "THERE!" Everyone looked up. There was a collective gasp.

"Just like they said!" someone else shouted excitedly, "Just like they said!"

Indeed it was. The Second Temple had been taken by fire and now, after thousands of years of waiting, the Third Temple was arriving in fire. The rest, as the great Hillel said, is commentary.

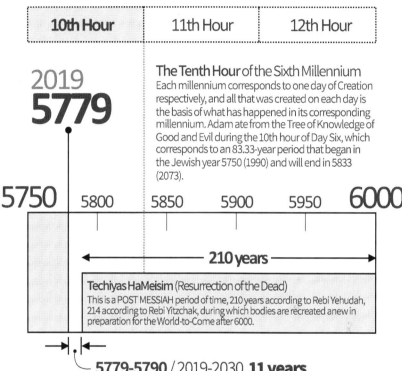

10th Hour	11th Hour	12th Hour

2019
5779

The Tenth Hour of the Sixth Millennium
Each millennium corresponds to one day of Creation respectively, and all that was created on each day is the basis of what has happened in its corresponding millennium. Adam ate from the Tree of Knowledge of Good and Evil during the 10th hour of Day Six, which corresponds to an 83.33-year period that began in the Jewish year 5750 (1990) and will end in 5833 (2073).

5750 | 5800 | 5850 | 5900 | 5950 | 6000

← 210 years →

Techiyas HaMeisim (Resurrection of the Dead)
This is a POST MESSIAH period of time, 210 years according to Rebi Yehudah, 214 according to Rebi Yitzchak, during which bodies are recreated anew in preparation for the World-to-Come after 6000.

→|.|←

5779-5790 / 2019-2030, **11 years**
Current History until Techiyas HaMeisim

This is the amount of time left until the beginning of Techiyas HaMeisim, by which time Messiah has to have come and **already** rectified the world.

The Last Quarter
based upon the book, "Need to Know"

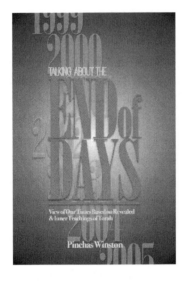 

Available in Softcover
and Kindle formats
through Amazon, and
PDF format through
Thirtysix.org.

THE FOLLOWING TITLES are all the books written over the years. Some books may no longer be in print, but many are still available in either PDF or Kindle formats. Visit the Thirtysix.org OnLine Bookstore, or Amazon for more information, or to order online.

If you order using AmazonSmile, each purchase will generate a contribution for Thirtysix.org. You just have to designate "Thirtysix Org Inc." as your charitable organization of choice, and Amazon will take care of the rest.

The Unbroken Chain of Jewish Tradition, 1985
The Eternal Link, 1990
If Only I Were Wealthy, 1992
If Only I Understood Why, 1993

If Only I Could See the Forest, 1993
If Only I Could Stay, 1993
If Only Great Was Greater, 1993
The Y Factor, 1994
Life's A Thrill, 1994
No Atheists in a Foxhole, 1994
Changes that Last Forever, 1994
The Making of a Great Jewish Leader, 1994
Bereishis: A Beginning With No End, 1994
The Wonderful World of Thirtysix, 1995
Redemption to Redemption, 1997
The Big Picture, 1998
Perceptions, 1998
Not Just Another Scenario, 2001
At The Threshold, 2001
Anticipating Redemption, 2002
Sha'ar HaGilgulim, 2002
Hadran (Hebrew), 2004
Talking About The End of Days, 2005
Talking About Eretz Yisroel, 2005
The Physics of Kabbalah, 2006
Be Positive, 2007
Geulah b'Rachamim, 2007
God.calm, 2007
Just Passing Through, 2007
On The Same Page, 2007
The Equation of Life, 2007
No Such Victim, 2009

Survival in 10 Easy Steps, 2009
Not Just Another Scenario 2, 2011
All In Your Mind, 2011
The Light of Thirtysix, 2011
The Last Exile, 2011
Drowning in Pshat, 2012
Drown No More, 2012
Shas Man, 2013
The Mystery of Jewish History, 2013
Survival Guide For the End-of-Days, 2013
Deeper Perceptions, 2013
Chanukah Lite, 2015
The Hitchhiker's Guide to Armageddon, 2016
Purim Lite, 2016
Pesach Lite, 2016
The Torah Empowerment Seminar, 2016
Siman Tov (Hebrew), 2016
The Fabric of Reality, 2016
Addendum, 2016
Fundamentals of Reincarnation, 2017
Reincarnation Clarified, 2016
All About Energy, 2017
What Goes Around, 2017
The God Experience, 2017
What in Heaven, 2017
The God Experience, Part 2, 2017
The God Experience, Part 3, 2017
It's About Time, 2017

Need to Know, 2017
Perceptions, Volume 2, 2017
Once Revealed, Twice Concealed, 2017
The Art of Chayn, 2017
A Matter of Laugh or Death, 2018
Geulah b'Rachamim Program, V. 1, 2018
Geulah b'Rachamim Program, V. 2, 2018
Geulah b'Rachamim Program, V. 3, 2018
Point of Acceptance, 2018
See Ya, 2018
In Discussion: Bereishis, 2018
Reincarnation Again, 2018
A Separate Matter, 2018
In Discussion: Shemos, 2019
A Search for Self, 2019
A Search for Trust, 2019
In Discussion: Bamidbar, 2019
How It Might Play Out, 2019

For more information regarding any of these books or other projects, write to pinchasw@thirtysix.org, especially if you are interested in making a dedication in an upcoming publication.

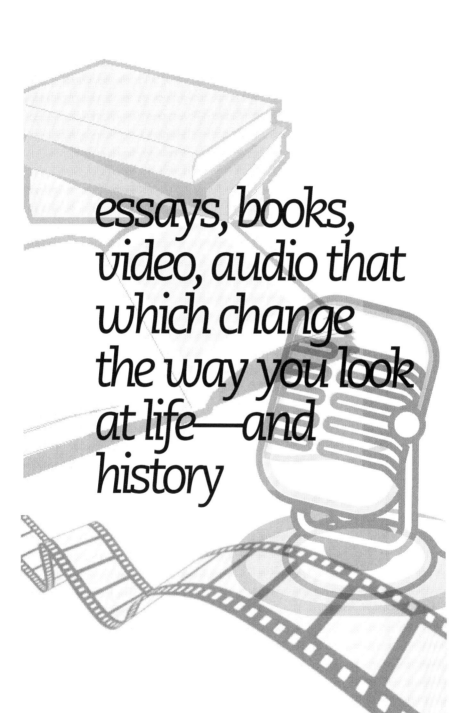

essays, books, video, audio that which change the way you look at life—and history

33370282R00142

Made in the USA
San Bernardino, CA
22 April 2019